A JiGGY McCUE STORY

THE TOiLET OF DOOM

MICHAEL LAWRENCE

ORCHARD

ORCHARD BOOKS
338 Euston Road, London NW1 3BH
Orchard Books Australia
Level 17/207 Kent Street, Sydney, NSW 2000

First published in 2001 by Orchard Books
This revised edition first published in 2009

ISBN 978 1 40830 404 4

Text © Michael Lawrence 2001/2009
Illustrations © Steve May 2009

A CIP catalogue record for this book is available from the British Library.
4 5 6 7 8 9 10

Printed in Great Britain

Orchard Books is a division of Hachette Children's Books,
an Hachette UK company.

www.hachette.co.uk

For Zelda
who shared the original Stallone
and typed thousands of doomed pages
in a small Welsh coastal town
without complaint

CHAPTER ONE

Ever had the feeling your life's been flushed down the toilet? I have. And it wasn't just a feeling. I knew something was wrong the moment I woke up that Sunday morning, but if I'd had the faintest idea *how* wrong I would have jumped straight out of the window on to my mother's favourite rose bush and ended it there and then.

Before I get to the Big Flush, though, I'd better fill you in on how it all started. It was the previous Friday – another day I woke up feeling something wasn't quite right. This time it was my nose. I rolled out of bed and plodded to the bathroom with dread in my heart. The mirror over the basin told me everything I didn't want to know. There was a lump on my hooter the size of a satellite dish. 'Terrific,' I said, imagining the day's pathetic jokes at my expense. I left the bathroom.

Left it...tripped over something...landed nose-first in a big potted plant on the landing.

The day was not starting well.

I pulled my face out of the leaves to see what had tripped me. Our cat, Stallone, lay across the doorway like a draught excluder. He must have seen me go into the bathroom and thrown himself across the door to catch me on the way out. Never misses a chance to trip me up, that cat. Me or Dad. Never trips Mum. He's nice as pie to her. Any female actually. My mother says he's a woman's cat. Dad says they're welcome to him.

'You did that on purpose, you…you…*animal.*'

Stallone stared back at me with those mean green eyes of his as if to say, 'Wanna make something of it, pal?'

The worst of it was the potted plant. It had only been there since yesterday and suddenly, day two, half its leaves and earth were on the carpet. Mum would go berserk. I got up and raced to my room.

I rummaged under the bed, found what I was looking for. At last I had a good use for my Maths exercise book! While I was down there I grabbed the ball of chewing gum I'd been building up piece by piece for months. I licked the fluff off and jammed it in my mouth to soften it. It tasted like the inside of a fisherman's boot, but I wasn't rearing it for a taste contest. Another couple of months and my gumball would have been big enough to break some sort of record. Would have. If Stallone hadn't made me use it to stick leaves back on a potted plant.

I was on my knees scooping earth back in the pot with my trusty Maths book when Dad strolled along the landing in his boxer shorts and "I'm not old, I'm a recycled teenager" T-shirt.

'What happened?'

I took the softened gumball out of my mouth. It wasn't easy. Almost broke my lips.

'Tripped over cat, fell in plant.'

'Your mum'll crucify you.'

'Only if we have a snitch in the family,' I said, starting on the leaves.

'She won't hear it from me, Scouts' honour.'

'You weren't in the Scouts.'

'What's that got to do with anything? Leaves fell off, did they?'

'Yeah. Sticking 'em back.'

'Chewing gum?' I nodded. 'Good move,' Dad said. 'Just what I'd have done.'

9

'When you were a kid, you mean?'

'I mean now. You know what the old girl's like with her rotten plants.' He noticed Stallone sprawling across the bathroom door and raised his foot. 'Gertcha!'

Stallone got up, glaring at him with real hatred, and slunk off lashing his tail like a whip.

'Jiggy, are you up yet?'

My mother's voice from downstairs. Dad shot into the bathroom and bolted the door. I looked down. Mum stood at the bottom of the stairs in her dressing gown, glaring up at me like I'd committed some crime. I had – the potted plant – but she didn't know that. Yet.

'On my way,' I said. She started up the stairs. Panic. There were still some leaves on the floor, and quite a bit of earth. 'I said I'm on my *way*!'

'And I'm coming up to get dressed, d'you mind?' she said.

I grabbed the leaves, crammed them in my mouth – useful things, mouths – chewed like a starving cow, swallowed hard. Then I scooped up the earth and dropped it in my pyjama trousers. It would have helped if I'd been wearing bicycle clips, but you don't usually get those with pyjamas. I headed downstairs, casually rubbing my nose.

'You'll be late,' Mum snapped, coming up.

'And good morning to you too,' I said, going down.

We drew near. It was going to be a close thing. Half the garden was trickling down my legs. My knees couldn't keep it off the ground for ever. But of course Mum stopped. Squinted at me.

'What's that on your nose? Looks like earth.'

'Earth?' I said. 'Well thanks very much. I mean I know it's big, but I didn't think it was the size of a *planet*.'

I carried on down, with no idea that the thing on my nose was going to be the one bright spot of my day. Next six days actually. By this time next week I would have been to hell and back.

Twice.

CHAPTER TWO

After breakfast I got dressed in time to be almost late for school as usual, said goodbye to my mother, wiped the lipstick mouth off my forehead, and strolled down the path.

'Mind the road,' she said from the step.

'Mother,' I said, walking backwards, 'this is the Brook Farm Estate. The only things on wheels round here are either parked or retired.'

'Still mind it. Someone gets run over every three minutes in this country.'

'He must get pretty sick of it,' I said, and crossed the road to Pete and Angie's.

Pete and Angie are my oldest buds. We've known one another since before we were born. They're not related to one another, but they live in the same house these days, along with his dad and her mum. We call ourselves The Three Musketeers (the kids, not the parents) and we have this Musketeery slogan, 'One for all and all for lunch!'

which we cry whenever we leap into action, which is a bit too often for my liking.

They came out seconds before I got to the door. We have this almost-late business down to a fine art. And of course, true to form, the first thing Pete said was: 'I like the nose, did you pick it yourself?'

I ignored him. Best thing to do with Pete most of the time. But Angie was looking too. You don't ignore Angie Mint. Not if you want to live.

'OK,' I said. 'Get it out of your system.'

'Get what out of my system?'

'The stupid remark about my conk.'

She looked offended. 'I'm offended,' she said.

'You are?' I said. 'Oh. Sorry.'

'I should think so too. I would never be so unkind as to make fun of a face that's been taken over by a giant plum tomato that probably glows in the dark.'

'Thanks, Ange.'

We set off for school.

'Oi, wait for me!'

We groaned. Eejit Atkins. Ralph to his mum, the teachers and social workers, Eejit to his dad and everyone else.

'We'll never get this right,' Angie muttered.

What she meant was that ever since Eejit moved in next door to me we've been trying to get to school without him on our heels and we usually don't make it. It's like he waits for us behind the Atkins family wheely bin and shoots out the moment we appear.

'Wotcher, Squirt,' said Pete.

Eejit gave him a kick in the shins and swerved so Pete couldn't get him back, then fell into step beside me. Since he became my neighbour he's been treating me like some long-lost relative. I don't encourage him. He chattered like a chipmunk halfway to school while Pete, Angie and I talked among ourselves, but then he caught sight of a couple of his Neanderthal pals loping along the opposite pavement and zigzagged across the road to join them.

Reaching school we jostled our way merrily through the gates. The school gates are about as wide as four kids standing shoulder to shoulder and at the start and end of every day at least sixteen people always want to get in or out at the same time. We broke through without too many personal injuries just in time for the bell, and headed for Registration.

Friday mornings aren't too bad at Ranting Lane School, but the afternoons are a real snoozefest. This is because the last two lessons of the week are RE with Mr Prior and Maths with Mr Dakin. We used to have History after lunch on Fridays, but they moved it so all the RE lessons could be at the end of the week and Prior wouldn't have to come in so often. Old Priory isn't a strong man. Kids make him twitch. He'd been off all week having a nervous breakdown at his mother's, which meant that other teachers had been standing in for him. And who did we get that Friday? Dakin.

Now Face-Ache Dakin is nobody's favourite. Besides being our miserable Maths teacher he's our miserable form tutor, which means that we see more of him than just about any other life-form on Earth. We do not burst into song every time we think of this. Even his son Milo doesn't like him much. Milo's in our class, and while his old man is Mr Grim, Mr Strict, Milo is one of the nicest kids there. Now that he was in charge of both last lessons Dakin Senior decided to change the order, Maths first, RE last. If he thought this would end our week on a high note he was even more off his twig than usual.

When the time came to switch to RE, Dakin called three of us out and pointed to a small brown suitcase he'd brought in with him.

'Skinner, Wapshott, Aziz, open that, divide up what you find inside, place a copy on every desk.'

We all threw our necks up on poles to see what was in the case, then took them off the poles when we saw. Books. Old books with black covers. Skinner, Wapshott and Aziz scooped them up and started strolling around dropping them on desks.

'Do not *drop* them!' Dakin yelled. 'They are not *litter*!'

They carried on dropping them, but more quietly, and as each book landed the person it was dropped in front of looked at the title and groaned.

'Yes, class,' Dakin said: 'Bibles. King James's Bibles.'

'Won't he miss them, sir?' I said.

'The Bibles you are used to,' he went on, 'are modern mass-market translations. The language in them is dull, flat, uninspiring. These, on the other hand...' He stroked the cover of the one on his desk. 'You are about to have an experience denied most of today's children. You are going to hear the words of the Bible as they should be heard. Speak them as they should be spoken.'

I tipped my chair back and spoke over my shoulder to Milo.

'What's the old crackpot up to, Milo? Why the ancient Noddy books?'

'He's been longing for a chance to show these off,' Milo said. 'They used to be in my barmy Aunt Trixie's religious bookshop. Been under the bed in our spare room ever since it was turned into a Chinese takeaway.'

'Why was your spare room turned into a Chinese takeaway?'

'You two, stop talking!' Dakin bawled. I faced front. 'So rich is the language in this Bible,' he said more quietly, 'that I haven't even chosen a section for us to look at.'

'Can we go home now then?' Bryan Ryan asked.

'I haven't chosen a particular section because I know that I can open it at any point – anywhere at all – and find something uplifting, something poetic, something—'

'Boring?' said Ryan.

'Detention, Ryan,' said Dakin.

'Wicked,' said Ryan, grinning round like a hero.

'I shall demonstrate.' Face-Ache flipped open the Bible on his desk. 'Here we are, a completely random selection. Second Book of Kings. Turn to page four-two-five, everyone.'

Lots of rustling paper.

'Turn to it with *care*. These pages are delicate.'

Lots more rustling. *Lots* more. With any luck we could stretch it out to the end of the lesson.

'Have you all got it?' Dakin said wearily after ten minutes' rustling.

'What page, sir?' Atkins asked.

'Four hundred and twenty-five.'

'Twenty-five?' said Hislop.

'Yes,' said Dakin.

'Four *hundred* and twenty-five?' said Pete, who sits next to me.

'Yes!' said Dakin. 'What is the *matter* with you people?'

'Well since you ask I think I've got a cold

coming,' someone said.

'Me too,' said someone else. 'My nose keeps running.'

'Why don't you put it in a race then?' another dumbo chipped in.

'McCue's got a jammy doughnut on the end of *his* nose,' said Ryan.

'ENOUGH!' Dakin screamed. 'Now if you've all managed to find the page, I want each of you to stand up and read a verse in turn.'

A class-wide groan. 'Oh, not reading *aloud*!'

'Yes, reading aloud. Starting at the front here with you, Julia.'

'Me?' gasped orange-haired, orange-freckled Julia Frame. 'Can't someone else go first?'

'Someone else can go *second*,' Face-Ache said firmly. 'Chapter nine, verse one. Arise and begin.'

Julia clunked to her feet. She was about to start reading when a phone rang.

Dakin's shoulders went up. His eyes shrank to pinheads.

'WHOSE IS THAT?!'

Six boys stood up at once, not to admit the phone was theirs, but to point dramatically at Pete,

19

who was fumbling in his pocket trying to turn the thing off. There'd been so many punishments for bringing mobiles into school that hardly anyone did any more, but Pete loves his phone. He doesn't get many calls but he still loves it.

'Garrett, how many times do you have to be *told*? Bring that thing here!'

Pete got up. Took the mobile out of his pocket. It was still ringing.

'And *silence* it!'

Pete punched a button. The ringing stopped. He put the phone to his ear and headed for the front. 'Yeah? Who? No, wrong number. Get lost.' He clicked off.

Dakin snatched the phone and chucked it in a drawer. 'Detention, Garrett.' Pete sauntered back to his seat. 'Now Julia, chapter nine, verse one. And read *clearly* please.'

Julia looked at the Bible, started to mumble.

'I said *clearly*,' Dakin said.

'This *is* clearly,' said Julia.

'Not to my ears, it isn't.'

'You can get them syringed at the Med Centre, sir,' I said. 'Doesn't hurt, just blows your brains out.'

'McCue should know, sir,' Pete said. 'He's had it done twice.'

'Start again,' Dakin said to Julia. 'And let us *hear* you this time.'

Julia started again. We couldn't hear a word, but no one complained, not even Face-Ache until she started the next verse.

'Just verse one, Julia. Angela?'

Angie stood up. She sits next to Julia. Pete and I grinned at one another. No chance of missing verse two with old Ange reading. Her mouth's got a built-in megaphone.

'"And when thou comest thither",' she bawled, '"look out there Jehu the son of Je-hosh-a-PHAT, the son of Nim…Nimi…Nimshi, and go in, and make him arise up from—"'

'*What* sort of language did he say this was?' someone muttered.

Soon, though, it had become a pretty smooth operation. When someone finished reading their verse and sat down, the next person crashed to his or her feet and read theirs, while the rest of us tried to keep the snores down. Dakin was standing at the window with his hands behind his back by this time. If I did that in class he'd ask my parents to come and see him.

Neil Downey got up to read his verse. '"And he arose, and went into the house; and he poured the oil on his head—"'

'Stupid thing to do,' said Ryan.

I looked at the next verse but one, which would be mine. I looked again. And gulped. Why me? I thought. Why *me*?

Downey sat down. Pete got up to do his bit.

'"And thou shalt smite the house of Ahab thy master, that I may avenge the blood of my servants the Muppets..."'

'I think you'll find that is "prophets", Mr Garrett.'

'Oh yeah. "And the blood of all the servants of the LORD, at the hand of, er...Jezebel?"'

He sat down. Silence fell. I hunched low in my chair, hoping Dakin wouldn't notice me.

'Up, McCue, up, keep it flowing, keep it flowing.'

A giggle from across the room. Someone had noticed my verse. Then someone else noticed. Then a low ripple started as more and more people checked it out. Then Pete saw it.

'Oh boy. Oh boy, oh boy, oh boy. This is gonna be *priceless*.'

'Can someone else do mine, sir?' I said. 'Bit of a sore throat today.'

'No excuses. On your feet, boy! Read!'

I got up. Cleared my throat.

'"For the whole house of Ahab shall perish",' I read, '"and I will cut off from Ahab him that pisseth against the wall, and him that is shut up—"'

Pete slid under his desk. The rest of the class exploded.

And guess who got detention for causing it.

CHAPTER THREE

When the bell went Ryan, Pete and I stayed
behind. There's a rule at our school that a kid can't
do a detention the day he gets it. Has to take a note
home to tell his parents he's been Bad and give
them a chance to nag him to death for a while.
Dakin wrote our notes with a few angry stabs of his
pen and threw them at us. 'Monday!' Ryan
sauntered out like he'd just won the lottery. Face-
Ache gave Pete his mobile back with a warning
that next time he'd be taken to the bike sheds
and shot.

Angie was waiting for us at the gates. Milo
Dakin was with her. Milo had been looking pretty
cheesed off all day and looked even cheesier now,
which was strange as it was home time.

'Why the face like a horse, Milo?' I said. 'Wasn't
you got detention.'

'I have detention every day of the week,' he said.
'You should try living with my dad.'

'I'd rather tattoo my chest with a power drill.'

Seeing as he was so down we went home his way instead of ours. Bit of a roundabout route but there was no rush. He moaned about his dad every step of the way and we made sympathetic noises to try and cheer him up. Well, Angie and I did. Pete kept rolling his eyes and jerking his head at us to try and get us to turn back and go home a non-Milo way.

'*Fat Chance*, ladies and gentlemen! *Fat Chance*! Help the homeless!'

An ultra-thin kid of about eighteen with a shaggy black dog shoved a magazine for the homeless in our faces. We reared back. Some days you can't move in our town without tripping over *Fat Chance* sellers and their dogs. They always have dogs.

'Got one,' I lied to the *Fat Chance* seller and his dog. 'At home.'

'Oh sure, and where've I heard *that* before?' muttered the *Fat Chance* seller.

'Woof-off,' said the dog.

'He's driving me bonkers,' said Milo as we walked on.

'Yeah, those *Fat Chance* sellers,' Pete said.

'He means his dad,' Angie said.

'I knew that. Just hoping he'd change the CD.'

Milo didn't change the CD. 'I don't know how much longer I can live my life in alphabetical order,' he said.

'Alphabetical order?' I said. 'How does that work then?'

'It's his latest "Keep Dakin World Tidy" scheme. Everything in my wardrobe and chest of drawers is already colour co-ordinated, but last night he word-processed all these labels saying "Handkerchiefs, Pyjamas, Shirts, Socks, Underwear". Does that sound *sane* to you?'

Angie patted him on the shoulder. 'Parents and teachers, Milo. Make it up as they go along. Don't let him get you down.'

These wise words didn't seem to help. Milo mooched on, dragging his school bag. This wasn't like him. He usually took his old man in his stride with a merry grin and a wince. It was hard to know what to say to him in this mood, so we just dragged our bags and mooched with him. It was Angie who broke the moochy silence.

'Just look at the state of that place. It's like

an Oxfam reject shop.'

I glanced at the big new luxury apartment building across the road. It had got a lot of people talking, that place, because no one knew who owned it. Some rich businessman, they said, who stood to make a killing but didn't want people to know. The flats weren't for sale, just rent, but a month's rent there would have probably bought our house and garden gnome.

'The luxury apartment block for filthy rich people looks like an Oxfam reject shop?' I said in surprise.

'I mean Mr Mann's bus shelter,' said Angie.

Mr Mann's bus shelter was on our side of the road, bang opposite the luxury apartment block. Mr Mann was the town tramp. He'd turned up out of nowhere five or six years earlier, spent the night in the bus shelter, and never moved out. Summer, winter, heatwave, snow, there he was. Never had a fire, even in really cold weather, just gloves, moth-eaten balaclava, string round his ankles.

'What I wouldn't give to take a broom and wheely bin to it,' Angie said.

'A match would be quicker,' said Pete.

It was a mess though, no denying it. Piles of old blankets and junk and litter, an ancient bookcase. Mr Mann was a great one for books. People gave him books all the time, and clothes and towels and stuff, though I don't think he ever asked. He had this thick tangled beard down to his waist, and thick tangled hair all down his back, tucked in the belt of his ratty old overcoat, which he wore in all weathers. But he was quite popular in spite of the way he looked and the state of his home. When the council tried to evict him last year there was a public outcry, so they dropped the idea and built a new shelter fifty metres along for people who actually want to catch buses.

'Hi, Mr Mann,' said Milo.

The raggedy old tramp looked up from his book and smiled.

'Hi, Milo. Good day at the workhouse?'

'Nah. You?'

'Oh, mustn't complain.'

Pete and Angie and I kept our eyes on the pavement. This wasn't our patch so we didn't know Mr Mann to speak to.

'You're very friendly with him,' Angie said when

the bus shelter was behind us.

'He's a nice man,' Milo said. 'I pass him twice a day, often stop for a natter.' He sighed. 'I envy him. No responsibilities, no one telling him what to do the whole time.' He sighed again. 'P'raps I should give the Toilet of Life a go. Never know, I might pick up a few tips on how to handle it. Life, I mean.'

'What's the Toilet of Life?' Angie asked.

'Computer game. I...I know the person who invented it.'

Pete whirled round, eyes on springs. 'You know someone who invents *computer games*?' It was almost a shout. Pete's a computer game nut.

Milo shrank back in alarm. 'He only does it in his spare time,' he said, like he'd just been accused of something. 'Just to keep his hand in. Used to be a scientist, something to do with genetics, but then he started his own games company, and...'

He stopped. Seemed kind of embarrassed about running off at the mouth, as if he was betraying some kind of trust. Pete wasn't interested in the background info anyway.

'This game, this Toilet of Life, what's it do?'

'I never played it,' Milo said. 'All I know is it's

something to do with swapping your life for a better one.'

'Which is why you're so tempted,' I said.

He grunted.

'But it's only a game, Milo,' Angie said. 'Won't change anything in the real world.'

'No, nothing changes that.' He sighed for the millionth time since we left school. 'You have no idea what it's like in our house. Can't relax. Ever. He's so fussy, so picky. Everything has to be so *right* all the time.'

'Just when I thought we'd got on to something worth talking about,' Pete muttered.

'I mean *exactly* right,' Milo went on, running the risk of boring us to tears. 'Like he doesn't believe in duvets so we have sheets and blankets, and I have to make my bed with the corners tucked under in perfect triangles, and my pyjamas have to be folded and smooth like they just came out of cellophane, and doors must be closed without a sound, and lights turned off when you leave the room for ten seconds, and he goes ballistic if I put my elbows on the table at mealtimes, and…and did you ever hear of anyone else who has to eat spaghetti with a knife and fork?'

'Doesn't sound much fun,' I said as we turned into Pizzle End Road and approached the Dakin residence.

'It isn't,' he said. 'Used to drive Mum even crazier than me. I'm not surprised she walked out. Just wish she'd taken me with her, that's all.'

'Poor old Milo,' Angie said. But it was getting a bit of a strain even for her.

We reached his gate, and Pete and Angie and I raised our hands in farewell. They were still in the air when Milo spoke again.

'And proper names,' he said.

We lowered the farewell hands. 'Proper names?' I said.

'Another rule. Proper names have to be used at all times. Full names. No abbreviations, no nicknames or initials. Like for instance a TV can't be called a TV in our house, oh no.'

'So what do you call it,' Pete said, 'a fridge?'

'A fridge is a "refrigerator" and the TV is the "television". If I ever call it a telly he hits the roof.'

'The roofateria,' said Pete.

'He probably just wants you to grow up

appreciating the real names of things,' said Angie, not meaning a word.

Milo shook his head. 'He was the same with Mum. She had to use the right words too. Everything had to be done the way he said. House had to be spotless the whole time, perfect, in case anyone visited.'

'And did they?' I asked.

'Did they what?'

'Visit.'

'Who?'

'Visitors.'

'No,' said Milo. Pause. Then he said: 'He wouldn't even let her have a dishwasher.'

'The brute,' said Angie, and we left him to it before he could get started on life without a dishwasher.

CHAPTER FOUR

Saturday morning. Fell out of bed and headed for the bathroom to see what the distorting mirror over the basin had to offer. Nothing good. The growth on my snoz had doubled in size overnight. Soon I'd need a periscope to see over it. But I couldn't burst it. If I burst it I might be scarred for life. Besides, Mum would be in a mood for hours when she saw the mess on the mirror.

As I left the bathroom I met Dad yawning along the landing. I hadn't told him or Mum about Face-Ache's detention yet because I'd been waiting to get him on his own. When Mum hears I've been in trouble at school she comes over all disappointed and hurt like I'm letting her down personally or something, but Dad can usually handle it. Mum says this is because he's still a big kid himself.

'Hey, Dad,' I said. 'You know you're always saying how you used to get detentions at school all the time?'

'Ah yes.' His eyes misted over. 'Happiest days of my life.'

'Well I got one yesterday. In RE.'

'Detention in RE? How'd you manage that? Even I never had one of *those*.' He sounded impressed. 'What about love thy neighbour?'

'Doesn't apply to teachers and kids. I've got a note.'

'A note?'

'From Mr Dakin to tell you I'm in detention after school on Monday. You have to sign it.'

'Forge my signature, you know how it goes. So what did you do? This I have to hear.'

I told him. The exact words.

He smirked. 'How things have changed.'

I stroked the luminous Himalaya on my nose. 'Changed?'

'Since biblical days. Must have been pretty common back then, pissething against walls. Nowadays we pisseth in lavatory pans, and flusheth afterwards.'

And he went into the bathroom to do just that. I went back to bed.

An hour later Mum threw my door back. She wasn't happy.

'Jiggy, your father tells me you've been given a detention! And in RE of all things!'

I covered my head with the pillow. Stupid. Didn't swear Dad to secrecy. Mum tugged the pillow away and leaned over me with a hefty scowl.

'Well? What do you have to say for yourself?'

'I say it wasn't my fault. I only did what I was told.'

'Oh. Really. And I suppose you got detention for no reason.'

'Yes,' I said. 'Absolutely. Glad you understand.'

'All I understand,' she said, 'is that you're grounded for the day.'

'The day? Today? But Mum, it's Saturday!'

'Yes it is, and you will spend it catching up on all the homework you've so conveniently forgotten.'

'But that'll take *years*!'

'Better get started then. And if you don't finish it to my satisfaction today you'll work on it tomorrow too.'

I managed to drag out most of the morning by eating breakfast and getting dressed in slow motion, but by early afternoon Mum had cottoned on to my cunning scheme and marched me up to

35

my room and thrown my school books at me. So there I was, Saturday afternoon, day of rest number one, slaving away in my room and wondering how close I was to dying of boredom. I had my music up really loud to drown out the racket from downstairs. Dad was watching football down there, and when my dad's watching football the last place you want to be is the same house, or even the same street. I looked at the clock on the wall. Five to twelve, it said. Time was really dragging, mainly because the batteries had been dead for weeks. I got up, moved the hands to five past three. 'Hmm,' I said, 'mid-afternoon. Time to raid the biscuit tin and knock back a litre or two of fizz.'

I headed downstairs.

The noise got more and more unbelievable with every downward step. It was hard to tell who was making the most, the telly or Dad. As I jumped the last three stairs my lunatic father gave a yell so terrifying that I twitched in mid-air and fell in my second potted plant in as many days. Fortunately, this one was plastic. I picked it up, put it back on the stupid little plastic plant table, and looked in the living room. There he was, the poor old Golden

Oldie, shouting and punching the ceiling. Braindead United had scored. I was surprised to see that he wasn't alone today. Stallone was there too. Stallone usually makes himself scarce when football's on, like me when I have a choice – like my mother, who'd gone to the Garden Centre where she practically lives. But today Stallone was in and he didn't look too pleased about the peace-and-quiet famine.

Before I go any further I'd better tell you how we came to be the proud owners of a cat like Stallone. Before him, we'd only had one pet. A budgie. We got the budgie because one day Mum said she needed someone sensible to talk to. Dad was happy enough about the budgie plan because budgies don't cost a lot. He got less happy in the pet hypermarket, though, when he realised that you can't buy a budgie without also buying a budgie cage, a budgie bell, a budgie mirror, a budgie ladder, and some millet. But it was too late to back out by then because Mum had fallen in love with this cute little blue fella. Dad wanted to call him Schwarzenegger but Mum preferred Beaky. Mum won, as usual. Beaky turned out to be the perfect name as it happens, but we didn't know that at the time. Beaky the Blue Budgie had only been with us a couple of days when Bella and Archie, my grandparents, turned up without an appointment. They brought us a present, something they thought we'd really like: a half-wild alley cat. One look at those hard green eyes and that bristling fur and Dad said, 'Stallone. We're going to call him Stallone.' The new addition to the McCue household bared his teeth and spat at him. Dad spat back. It was hate at first sight. But next morning Stallone seemed more relaxed. Pretty pleased with himself too. Wasn't hard to see why. Beaky's cage was empty. All that was left of our poor little birdie was a few blue feathers waving about in the budgie droppings at the bottom. And his beak, clinging to the bars.

Anyway. Saturday afternoon, Stallone home, Dad bawling at the box. You could tell Stallone didn't appreciate the commotion by the way he stood, ears up, eyes like killer zap guns aimed at the middle-aged yob on the couch. Dad wasn't aware of the effect he was having on the family pet. Too busy jumping up and down and screaming himself hoarse, arms in the air.

But then Stallone cracked. With an ear-splatting squeal of rage the furious cat flew across the room, landed on the innocent football fan's chest, and drove his claws deep into the armpits on either side. Dad's new scream wasn't much different from the old one except there was a tad less joy in it. The mad moggy must have sensed that he'd overstepped the mark because the scream was still bouncing around the walls when he raced back across the room and jumped out the window.

'That's it!' Dad shrieked. 'That cat is going to the vet's!'

I went to the window. 'No, he's going the other way.' But then I realised what he meant. I turned in horror. 'Dad, you wouldn't.'

He looked from one armpit to the other. Blood was seeping through his shirt. 'Watch me,' he growled.

'You can't,' I said. 'I mean yes, OK, he went a little over the top just then, but that's no reason to have him put down. Couldn't you just, say…cut his meat ration for a while?'

Dad looked up from his armpits. His eyes were

almost as red as they were. He gave a dry little chuckle like a warped genius who's just worked out how to destroy the world and make a profit.

'I won't have him put down. Too good for him. No. I'll have him done.'

'Done?'

'Neutered. Doctored. Separated from his cherries. If that doesn't calm him down, nothing will. It'd certainly take the edge off my day.'

But then a dim little spot of sanity returned to his eyes.

'Don't tell your mother though, will you? She wouldn't approve.'

'You told her about my detention.'

He looked suddenly shifty. 'I had to. Can't keep school stuff from your mum, you know that. Has to know how you're doing all the time. And I didn't tell her what you did to her plant, did I?'

'Only because a miracle occurred and she didn't notice. Anyway that wasn't my fault. Stallone tripped me.'

'Stallone again,' Dad said. 'You have to admit, that cat's a liability. If we have him seen to he'll be calmer. Less mean. Come on, Jig, say you won't tell your mum Stallone's heading for the nutcracker.'

'She's bound to find out sooner or later,' I said. 'Probably next time he rolls on his back with his legs all over the place.'

The mad look flashed back into his eyes. A thin tight smile jerked his lips to left and right.

'By then it'll be too late. The little monster'll be as docile as a fluffy pyjama case.'

With that he fell back on the couch looking from one bloody pit to the other, and began whimpering quietly. Something happened on the telly that turned the crowd hysterical. Dad didn't hear. Didn't notice.

CHAPTER FIVE

Angie helped me with my homework for a couple of hours. On the phone. She's better than me at Maths, Science, History, Geography and Woodwork Theory. When Mum returned from the Garden Centre and found Dad whingeing on the couch, she drove him to the hospital for a tetanus jab. Dad usually drives when they go out together but she thought he might have a bit of a problem with his arms sticking out of the sun-roof. When she brought him back his arms were down but they still wouldn't hang properly because the bandages in his armpits were the size of bricks. Dad came up and looked in on me, still hard at work with Angie on my rotten homework.

'Has the vicious little fiend come back yet?'

'Haven't seen him. Probably keeping out of your way.'

'Very wise,' said Dad, and went.

'What was that all about?' Angie said in my ear.

'Tell you later.'

I was all set to slip over to hers and Pete's after tea when my mother threw herself across the front door.

'Oh no you don't, my lad. Grounded I said and grounded I meant.'

'Until I caught up with my homework, you said.'

Her face went all narrow and suspicious. 'Are you saying you have?'

'Absolutely, now move aside please.'

'You're not leaving this house until I've checked it over.'

'The house?'

'The homework. If it's not up to scratch you can do it again.'

'Oh very funny,' Dad said, leaning out of the living room.

'What did I say?' Mum asked.

'Up to *scratch*!' he said, and slammed the door.

Mum armlocked me up to my room and went through my homework. Went through it so slowly the hands on my dead clock moved faster. She made me do a couple of bits again too, so it was getting late by the time I was finally allowed out.

Over the road I rang Pete and Angie's bell. Pete and Angie's bell is black-and-white plastic, like all the others on our side of the estate. On the other side – over on Madonna Way and Brad Pitt Close – the bells are solid brass. They also have four bedrooms, double garages and better wheely bins. You don't like to stand in the street for more than two seconds over there in case you get dragged off as litter.

Pete opened the door. He had a can of non-Diet something in his fist.

'Hi, scumbag.'

'Whose room?' I said, barging past him.

'Mine.'

We started up the stairs. 'Where's Angie?'

'Bath, hairwash. Usual Saturday night girlie stuff. Coming along a treat, that.'

'What is?'

'The giant fairy light on your nose.'

Up in his room he flopped into the swivel chair in front of his PC.

'What are you doing?'

'Writing my diary,' he answered, typing.

'You keep a diary? You've never said. What do you put in it?'

'All the really terrific and exciting stuff that happens round here.'

He leaned back so I could read what he'd just written.

Saturday. Did nothing. Evening. Jiggy here. Typed this.

'And these are the best years of our lives,' I said sadly.

'Hey – life!' Pete said.

'What about it?'

'That game Milo mentioned. The Toilet of Life. Let's check it out.'

I'm not into computer games myself, but there wasn't really anything else to do, so I said: 'OK.' And with those two simple letters – O and K – I sealed my fate. If I'd had any idea what was going to happen I would have run from that room, that house, and locked myself in our garden shed till Christmas. But I didn't run. I waited while Pete typed 'Toilet of Life' in the search window. And there it was. Then he clicked something and a door appeared. A notice on the door said 'Vacant'.

'What now?' I said.

Pete clicked the notice. The door swung inward

and we were looking at a large toilet with the seat down. Scrawled on the wall behind the toilet, like graffiti, were the words:

The Toilet of Life
A Manx Game

There were no instructions, no clues what to do next, so Pete clicked around a bit more. Nothing happened until he clicked on a little handle. The handle moved, the toilet flushed, and suddenly the screen was chock-a-block with much smaller toilets, all with their seats down. Not just toilets though. Walking round them, weaving in and out of them, were all these little people – men in suits, women in skirts, OAPs with walking sticks, kids blowing bubble gum – all sorts, like you see in any street.

'Interesting,' said Pete.

'It is?' I said.

'Let's see what happens next.'

He started clicking all over again. At first the result was the same as before – nothing – but then one of the tiny toilet seats flew up and the nearest little person gave a yelp and jumped head first into the bowl. He was halfway in, legs kicking wildly, looked stuck there, but then there was this miniature flushing sound and he slithered all the way down.

'How did you do that?' I asked.

'Dunno, but if I can do it once...'

He clicked away, searching for the hidden trigger that made the little people jump into the toilets and get flushed. A second seat flew up. A second little person yelped, jumped in, kicked, and was flushed away.

'Think I've got it,' Pete said, and clicked some more.

A third seat flew up, person three yelped, jumped in, got flushed. Pete gave a whoop. He got busy.

'Hey Jig.'

I turned with relief as Angie came in. Her hair was up in a towel and she was wearing shiny black pyjamas covered in stars and planets and comets and stuff.

'Hey Ange. Cool PJs.'

She plucked at the shiny black material. 'Cool?'

'Don't you like them?'

'If I had an ambition to be launched into space as a satellite I'd be over the moon about them, but as I don't...'

'So why are you wearing them?'

'Because my mother bought them specially. From a catalogue, sight unseen.' She gave me that long-suffering look we use when our mothers splat into the conversation. 'What's he up to?' she said, glancing at Pete's screen.

'That game Milo Dakin was thinking of trying. The Toilet of Life.'

'Any good?'

'Nah. Just another zapfest. Death and destruction but with toilets.'

We looked for somewhere to sit. This is always a problem in Pete's room because he likes to decorate the carpet with clothes, comics and all sorts of junk which wouldn't have looked out of place in Mr Mann's bus shelter. The only other place to sit was the bed but you wouldn't catch us on that – Pete's disgusting feet had been in it – so we cleared a space on the floor and parked our back ends. While Pete flushed and whooped like a maniac in the corner I told Angie about Mad-Cat Stallone and my father's armpits.

'He says he's going to have him vetted,' I said. 'Stallone's privates are going to be toast.'

'Bit drastic.'

'Yeah, but it's his own fault. I mean if you're a cat and you live in someone's house, rent free, all meals included, own dirt tray, you can't go round shredding their armpits whenever you feel like it.'

'Personally I think he showed quite a lot of self-control,' Angie said.

'How do you work that out?'

'Well if I was a cat stuck in a room with your dad while he's watching footie I'd skip the armpits and go straight for the throat. That'd shut him up.'

'Come and look at this,' Pete said.

'We're not interested in people being flushed down toilets,' I said.

'The people are all flushed. Now another toilet's turned up, with a message.'

'What sort of message?'

'Come and see.'

We got up, schlepped across the room, looked at the screen. The people and all the little toilets had disappeared. Their place had been taken by a much bigger toilet, a twin of the one we'd found behind the 'Vacant' door. Wafting round it was a banner with these words:

Feel that your life has gone down the pan?
Well here's your chance to swap it
for a better one.
Just invite someone round who's really got
it made and hit 'F for Flush'!

'So this is what Milo meant,' I said.

'Yeah,' said Pete. 'And like he said, it's tempting. Very tempting.'

He stretched a finger towards 'F for Flush'.

'Leave it alone,' Angie said. 'We don't know what it is.'

'Yes we do,' he said. 'It's a harmless computer game.'

'Well, leave it just in case.'

But she was curious, and maybe she would have let him hit 'F for Flush' if he hadn't been interrupted by a shout from downstairs.

'Pete! Why haven't you washed up yet?'

Pete went to the door. 'Five minutes, Dad!'

'No minutes! It's your turn on the rota and it should have been done. Kitchen, rubber gloves, five seconds, or you're in the deep stuff!'

'Talk about timing,' Pete said. He started to leave, but came back. 'Nobody hit "F for Flush" while I'm gone – right?'

'Wouldn't want to,' Angie said.

Pete went. I leaned over his empty swivel. Peered at the toilet on the screen. The seat was quivering, like it was itching to open. My 'F for Flush' finger twitched. I didn't know it but I was seconds away from a fate I wouldn't wish on my worst enemy. Well no, that's not quite true. It would have made my year to see Bryan Ryan get what was going to happen to me.

'Don't, Jig,' Angie said. 'I have a funny feeling about this.'

'It's just a gimmick,' I said. 'Come on, let's give it a go.'

'It says "Feel that your life has gone down the pan". Your life isn't so bad.'

'Not so bad? With a homework tyrant for a mother, an armpit-eating cat, and a meteorite on

51

my nose? Swap with you any day.'

'At least you have a *father*,' Angie said.

'He's all yours,' I said, and hit 'F for Flush'.

The toilet seat flew up and a bright blue cloud shot out. The cloud fanned across the screen until it filled it, corner to corner, and then...

...it started spewing into the room.

'Impossible,' I said.

'Told you something would happen,' Angie said.

'Yeah, but it's a computer game. No computer game is so interactive it can come into the room.'

More and more of the blue stuff seeped out. We backed away.

'Didn't Milo say the friend who invented it used to be some sort of scientist?' Angie said.

'So?'

'So maybe he added something extra. Something to make it *really* interactive.'

We stopped backing away. Not because we wanted to but because the wall didn't seem to like the idea of us backing through it. We glanced towards the door. The blue cloud swirled between us and it.

'Only other way out is the window,' I said. The

cloud hadn't got that far yet.

'You mean drop down on to the rockery?' Angie said. 'There are some sharp stones in that rockery.'

'Better than being suffocated by this stuff.'

We headed for the window. Too late. The blue cloud got there first. We were trapped.

'When we get out of here,' Angie said, 'I want you to remind me to do something.'

'What?' I said.

'Remove your teeth with pliers one by one,' she said, 'and play conkers with your eyeballs.'

We were still standing there wondering what to do next when the two halves of the cloud joined up and covered us. It was like being in a blue fog. Seconds later, all these sparkly bits started appearing. Then they were bursting – pop-pop-pop – like thousands of tiny balloons. And when they burst...

'What a *smell*!' Angie said.

She was right. No nostril could survive that for long.

Pop-pop-pop.

'I'm out of here,' I said, groping for the door.

Instead of the door I found Angie, also groping.

We slapped one another's hands for a while, then yanked the door back and stepped outside. As we closed the door to keep the smell and the cloud in, the Toilet of Life flushed – loudly. We stumbled downstairs, ripped the front door open, and gulped air.

'What's with you two?'

Pete stood behind us in yellow rubber gloves ten sizes too big for him, dripping all over the floor. We ignored him, carried on gulping.

'Hello, what's this?' Not Pete this time. Angie's mother Audrey.

'Terrible smell,' Angie said. 'In Pete's room.'

'Don't look at me, I wasn't even there,' Pete said.

Now Oliver, his father, joined us. It was turning into quite a party.

'What was that about a smell? Not gas?'

'Bit like it,' I gasped.

Oliver frowned. 'Could be gas. New house, cowboy builders...'

'Better go and look,' Audrey said.

'Me?' he said.

'Well you're the man.'

'Oh, I see. So it's all right for me to get blown to

smithereens, being a man, but not you, being a woman.'

But up he went, knowing he'd never hear the last of it if he didn't. Pete's dad and my dad have a lot in common.

'Feel sorta queasy,' Angie said quietly.

'So do I,' I said. 'And...sleepy.'

Oliver reappeared on the landing. He looked relieved. 'Not gas. Hardly any smell at all. Just the famous Pete Garrett foot-rot aroma.'

Angie yawned. 'Anything else there? Like a sparkly blue cloud?'

'Not that I noticed. Just this jazzy sort of pattern on Pete's computer.'

'What have you *done*?!' Pete said, and flew upstairs in his outsize rubber gloves.

'Gotta hit the sack,' Angie said.

'Me too,' I said.

She set off up the stairs, clawing the banister. I stumbled out into the street wishing I had a banister to claw. In two minutes I was home, up in my room. In three I was hopping about trying to slot a foot into a pyjama leg. In four and three-quarter minutes I was in bed. In five I was sleeping peacefully. Well, not so peacefully. I had a dream. A dream that I was being pulled down into this enormous toilet by grasping hands.

And flushed away.

CHAPTER SIX

And now we come to the morning it all *really* started. I woke up feeling kind of strange. Not myself somehow. But at least it wasn't a school day. Mum wouldn't be yelling for me to get up, not for a while anyway. She couldn't leave me entirely in peace though. It really annoys my mother when people are in bed and she's not. My head was deep inside the duvet, along with the rest of me, when I heard her voice somewhere on the other side of it.

'Jiggy, your father's gone to watch two-a-side football and I'm off to the Garden Centre to look at water features. Don't lie there all day.'

I waited for the front door to slam before heading for the bathroom to make a water feature of my own. I still felt sort of peculiar, like part of me was...well, missing. One thing that was definitely missing was the growth on my nose. Good news, I thought, stroking my smooth lump-free beak.

I was almost at the bathroom when I caught a sly movement on the stairs. Stallone – creeping up towards me. First I'd seen of him since yesterday. He'd probably slept in some alley to keep out of Dad's way. But he was back now, and looking at me. A shiver of fear tap-danced through me. Perhaps the great armpit massacre had given him a taste for human blood. Perhaps he wanted some of mine now. But he didn't attack me. Far from it. When he got to the top of the stairs he wound himself round my ankles; wound so tight I couldn't go another step. And purred. If you knew Stallone you'd know how rare this is. Purring just never happens, not when he's near me or Dad. But I saw what he was after. He wanted to get me on his side.

'It won't work,' I told him. 'I have no sympathy for you. You have only yourself to blame, only yourself.'

I eased my ankles out of his tight furry grip to stop myself going downstairs before I was ready, and continued along the landing for twelve full centimetres before I heard what I'd just said and came to a shocked halt. Well not *what* I'd said, but *how*. What was wrong with my *voice*?

The phone on the wall rang. I considered ignoring it, but it kept on ringing so I grabbed it to shut it up.

'What!'

'Jiggy?'

'Who's that?' I said with my new peculiar voice.

'Angie.'

'You don't sound like Angie.'

'You don't sound like Jiggy. We have to meet. Come to the door.'

'The door?'

'Tall white plasticky thing at the front of your house.'

'Soon as I'm dressed,' I said.

'*Come as you are!*' she yelled, busting an eardrum. '*NOW!!!*'

The phone died. I looked at the receiver. I had no interest in the receiver, but in films and on telly people always look at telephone receivers when the person at the other end hangs up. I've never understood this. I mean, what do they think it's going to do – apologise?

I jogged downstairs. I've done this a million times but today it felt all wrong, like my lower

59

decks had gone to the Bahamas without me.

I looked at the closed front door. Nervously. The front door is not one I often open in my pyjamas. This is mainly because pyjama bottoms have a way of springing apart just as the whole world walks by with a bulldog. I snatched a picture of my gran off the wall and put her over my fly. I opened the door. Across the road Pete and Angie's door was already open. Someone stood there looking at me. Someone in snazzy black pyjamas with stars and planets all over them. Not Angie though. Someone else.

Me.

I clutched the door handle to stop my knees giving way. As I clutched, I half turned and caught a glimpse of myself in the mirror which hung on the wall next to where my gran's picture wasn't.

The face in the mirror wasn't mine.

It was Angie's.

I looked back across the road. At myself in Angie's fancy PJs. I was puzzled. Too puzzled for the moment to be horrified. Horror would start about twenty-five seconds later when it sank in. Well I ask you. Would *your* mind be working on full power if you'd just woken up and discovered that you'd switched bodies with the kid across the road?

A kid of the opposite *sex*?

CHAPTER SEVEN

Angie and Pete came over ten minutes later. Angie had ditched the snazzy PJs, but the clothes she'd put on instead looked all wrong, because they were a girl's and the body wasn't. I hadn't got dressed. Hadn't been time. I'd spent the first six minutes gulping at the mirror and the other four dealing with an emergency in the bathroom.*

Naturally Pete found it all a real hoot. Mentality of a gnat, that boy. It was all right for him, he still had his own body, but it was no picnic for me having to walk round with Angie Mint's girlie apparatus. You don't need Sex Education lessons to know there are serious differences between boys and girls. Actually, knowing all the gory details made it even worse somehow. I'd seen the diagrams. I'd read the labels. I'd looked at the pictures of the internal workings with a magnifying glass. All the boys had. But now that I was so close to everything, using it like it was my own, I felt kind of...unwell.

---

* I won't go into that if you don't mind.

I soon found out that Angie didn't feel much happier, even though she had the better end of the deal.

'This is your fault,' she said, with my voice.

'How do you make that out?' I said, with hers.

'Well it wasn't me who hit "F for Flush".'

'You think the Toilet of Life did this?'

'Can you think of anything else that's invited you to swap lives with the person standing next to you recently?'

'Lives,' I said. 'Didn't say anything about bodies.'

'Same difference. I told you not to fiddle with it, but would you listen? Oh no.'

'Lynch him,' said Pete.

'Thanks, Pete,' I said.

'Guillotine him,' he said. 'Shoot him,' he added. 'Bung him in a bag and drop him in the river. Send him to the electric chair.'

'Electric toilet might be more appropriate,' I said.

'Please don't say that word,' said Angie.

'Electric?' I said. 'Appropriate?'

'Toilet.'

'You don't want me to say toilet?'

63

'No.'

'Why, what's wrong with "toilet" all of a sudden?'

'Just don't say it, all right?'

'OK, I won't say toilet again.'

'Make sure you don't.'

'Not a single toilet shall pass these lips. Not one toilet.'

'It *keeps* passing your lips. My lips.'

'Toilet? Does it?'

'Will you shut up? I'm almost wetting myself here.'

'So why don't you go to the toilet?'

She aimed a swipe at my head. I ducked just in time.

'I wonder,' said Pete.

We looked at him, shocked. It's not often Pete wonders.

'Wonder what?' I asked.

'If the Toilet of Life could be some new kind of computer virus.'

'Computer viruses ruin your hard disk, not your life. Corrupt your files, not your genes.'

'Yeah, but technology's advancing all the time.

Never know what they'll come up with next. If it is a virus that can travel round the Internet and infect people through their home computers…wow, talk about progress!'

'*Progress?*' Angie and I said, gazing helplessly at our bodies on the wrong people. 'Well, progress or not,' she said then, 'until we figure out what to do about it we have to pretend to be each other.'

'Why do I have to pretend to be one of you?' Pete asked.

'Not you, you wally. Come on,' she said to me. 'Upstairs. We have to swap clothes.'

'You want to swap *clothes* with me now?' I said in dismay.

'Looking the way we do, we have to,' she said.

We went up. Pete too, chuckling quietly.

'I think we need a few ground rules in case we can't reverse this for a while,' Angie said as we reached the landing.

'What sort of ground rules?'

'No peeking for one. That's my private property you have there, copyright Angie Mint. If you have to get changed in daylight or with the light on keep your eyes on the ceiling. No taking baths or

65

showers either. At last you have a genuine excuse. You only do stuff you really have to, and you don't hang about doing that. Got it?'

'Got it,' I said, 'and ditto.' We went into my room. 'In fact double ditto. You have one extra little attachment I wish I didn't have to mention.'

'The reason boy jelly babies are more popular than girl jelly babies,' Pete said.

'What are you on about?' Angie said.

'Get more for your money with the boys.'

She snarled. Turned to me.

'Clothes!'

I grabbed my things from the chair I'd thrown them at last night.

Angie curled my lip. 'Not *used* ones.'

'I was never that picky when I was a boy,' I said, but opened some drawers and hauled out a clean shirt, jeans, socks, Y-fronts.

'You can keep the undies,' she said.

'It's all right,' I said, 'they're new. My mother bought six pairs of fire-damaged pants from this vandalised warehouse sale. Besides, you have to wear some. They're specially designed to cope with the free extra attachment.'

'The escape route comes in handy,' Pete said.

Angie snatched the clothes, including the fire-damaged Ys, and flung herself out of the room. I flung myself after her.

'Where are you going?'

'Bathroom. To change.'

'I've seen it all before, you know. Quite often actually.'

'Not on me, you haven't.' She was about to go in when she thought of something. 'Jig, you haven't…you know, been to the…?'

'Had to,' I said. 'Don't worry, I sat through the whole thing.'

She slammed the door. Half a minute later it opened a fraction and I was leaping in all directions trying to catch the clothes she slung out.

'Clean on fifteen minutes ago,' she said, and slammed the door again.

Clean or not, she could keep the girlie undies. There was a limit. I carried them to my room between finger and thumb and kicked them into the Twilight Zone under my bed. Pete watched my every move, grinning like the village idiot.

I pointed at the door. 'Out!'

He went, chortling.

I got dressed. As quickly as I could with my eyes shut. I'd had about twenty minutes to get used to this by now but I still couldn't believe it was happening. I mean, imagine. There you are a boy all your life, you hit the hay one night and next morning there's a lot of slack in the fire-damaged Y-fronts. Something like that takes a bit of mental adjustment.

When Angie came out of the bathroom in my clothes she marched straight up to me and swiped me round the head again. This time she got me.

'What was *that* for?' It might have been her head but it was me who felt it.

She pointed angrily at her new nose.

'Oh, that,' I said.

The thrill of finding I'd turned into a girl in my sleep had put the spot quite a way down my list of things to get het up about. I gave it a look. It was so big today, so red and squishy, that you couldn't call it just a spot any more. No.

'It's a boil,' I said.

'Very big boil,' said Pete.

'Big as a house,' I said.

'Detached,' said Pete.
'And guess what, Ange,' I said.
'What?' she said.
'It's all yours.'

CHAPTER EIGHT

We considered telling our parents what had happened. But not for long. You can't tell your Golden Oldies you've swapped bodies with a neighbour and expect them to carry on as normal. Their poor old brains can't handle stuff like that. No, this was something we had to deal with ourselves.

'We need to think this through,' I said. 'But not here. I don't know what I'd do if Mum or Dad waltzed in and saw me like this.'

'They'd think you were me,' Angie said.

'Exactly. We need to be on neutral ground while we get used to this.'

'How about the park? Lots of neutral ground in the park.'

'Fine.'

'Have to be careful on the way though,' she said. 'Pretend we're who we look like in case we bump into anyone we know.'

'No problem for me,' said Pete.

'You mean if we meet someone I have to talk to them the way you would?' I said.

'Not just talk, you have to *be* me. If you look like me but act like you people will think something's up.'

'Something is up, Ange. Very up.'

'Yes, well let's stop whining and make the best of it, shall we?'

'Best?' I said. 'What best? There is no best.'

She came over all fierce. 'Pull yourself together, McCue. Where's your backbone?'

'Turn round, I'll show you.'

But I saw her point. If we didn't act like one another people might stare. Then they might start asking questions. Whatever happened we didn't want questions. Questions could make us a laughing stock. Two laughing stocks. We left the house and set off, trying to be each other. It wasn't easy. I mean I've known Angie since before I can remember, but I've never taken much notice of the way she moves and all. She seemed to be having a bit of trouble being me too.

'Angie,' I said, 'don't take this the wrong way,

but put a lid on the strut, eh? You're killing my image here.'

She narrowed my eyes at me. 'How do you mean?'

'Well Jiggy McCue's a pretty cool dude, and—'

'News to me,' said Pete.

'—and cool-as-a-cube Jig just doesn't walk like that.'

'So how am I walking that's so uncool?'

'Kind of hunched over and swinging my arms like something in a wildlife documentary with fleas. This isn't a criticism of you personally, you understand.'

'What about you then? You've started to mince.'

'Mince?'

'Walk with dear little steps and waggle my hips.'

'Get outta here.'

'He is, isn't he?' she said to Pete.

'Haven't noticed. Walk up and down,' he said to me.

'No.'

'Come on, man. Cause of science and all that.'

So I walked up and down a couple of times.

Pete nodded. 'Mincing like a maniac.'

'Look, I'm doing my best here,' I said. 'You think it's easy being a female?'

'Half the population seem to manage it,' Angie said.

'The other half. And will you stop doing *that*?'

'What now?'

'Pouting.'

'I do not pout!' she said, pouting like a porpoise.

'Didn't used to, not so I noticed anyway. Maybe my lips don't agree with you.'

'Don't get your knickers in a twist, Jig,' Pete said with a punchable smirk.

By this time Ange and I were doing our bad impressions of each other very close to the fateful spot where Milo had told us about the Toilet of Life. On the other side of the road was the block of luxury flats and on our side was Mr Mann's bus shelter.

'Wonder who he is?' Angie said.

'Mr Mann,' I said.

'I mean the bloke talking to him.'

The bloke talking to Mr Mann was an official-looking type in a suit who'd just taken a batch of papers out of his briefcase for Mr Mann to look through.

'Probably from the council,' Pete said. 'Sent to have another stab at getting him to sling his hook.'

'On a Sunday?'

'Overtime.'

The council type took a pen out of his pocket and handed it to Mr Mann, who scribbled something on one of the papers.

'Probably just signed his own eviction notice,' Angie said.

'Or death warrant,' said Pete.

'Hello, Angie, I've never seen you over this way before.'

We turned. It was Julia Frame of the orange hair and freckles who sits next to Angie in class. Julia really irritates Angie. Whenever she's in a mood Julia tries to cheer her up with hugs and little songs, and Angie wants to thump her. Suddenly I understood this. Here we are trying not to meet anyone we know and she pops up out of the blue with a bunch of flowers, smiling. At me.

'Shove off, Jools,' I said. 'We're having a private conversation here.'

Julia's sugar-sweet smile puckered. The flowers fell to her side.

'I only said hello.'

'Yeah, well who asked you to?'

Her forehead turned to corrugated paper. Her bottom lip trembled. 'Why are you always so mean to me?' she said miserably.

I glanced at the others. Pete was grinning his head off, but Angie was just watching, just listening. Her expression wasn't so easy to read, even though it was one of mine. Was that admiration I saw in my eyes? Maybe she was impressed. Thought I was doing a good job of being her.

'Mean?' I said to Julia. 'You ain't heard nothing yet. You want mean, stick around. If you don't, let's see your dust.'

A tear jumped into one of her eyes. She blinked. A tear jumped into her other eye. She blinked again. Then both tears jumped out and jogged down her cheeks.

'But I lent you my Barbie pencil sharpener.'

'And...?' I said.

'Well I don't lend just *anyone* my pencil sharpener.'

'I'm touched. Now beat it or I call the cops.'

A little sob burst like a bubble from her mouth. She spun round and walked away with her head about waist-high. I felt good about that for three whole seconds. Then I started feeling a bit less good. Then I came over guilty as hell. Pete's grin was even broader now. For some reason I couldn't look at Angie. I felt – don't laugh – ashamed.

'Hey Julia!' I yelled after her. 'Nice flowers! Who are they for?'

'They're for someone who *cares* about me!' she shouted back with a trembly voice. 'My Nan, for her birthday! She's over fifty, she'll be dead soon, then I'll be really upset and you can make even more fun of me!'

It was all I could do not to break down myself as she walked away. Me, Jiggy McCue, all set to blub his eyes out. Well, Angie's eyes. Hey now, wait. What was going on here? Angie never got all emotional about stuff, not soppy emotional, but I was using her equipment, so why had Julia got to me when she wouldn't have got to Ange? I needed to think about this, but not now. Now wasn't the time. I hauled a smirk on to my borrowed chops to cover my tracks.

'That girl's a nutter,' I said, super-cool.

I glanced at Pete, expecting him to agree with me. His grin was gone. He was gaping at me in horror.

'Nice *flowers*? Since when did you notice *flowers*?'

'Well I...'

He was right, of course. I'm a boy. Flowers live in another universe. I looked at Angie. Her expression was easy enough to read now. It told me that she knew what I was going through. Knew but wasn't sympathetic. Suddenly I realised something. Angie had all the emotional stuff that girls are born with but she didn't give in to it. She kept it inside, deep inside, refused to let it out. Looking at her now, head held high, shoulders back, you'd never have guessed she was a girl this time yesterday. She made a much better boy than I ever did.

CHAPTER NINE

It wasn't until we were almost at the park that I realised I wasn't living up to my name. I mean I'm not called Jiggy for nothing. For the first two or three years of my life I couldn't keep still for a minute. My parents thought there was something wrong with me. They took me to experts. The experts were stumped. Whatever they were expert in it wasn't perfectly healthy young kids who have to keep on the move without a break, day and night. Then they came to this Big Conclusion. 'He has too much energy, but he's too lazy to put it to proper use.' What they meant was that instead of doing normal boy stuff like getting into fights and kicking balls around between every meal I danced on the spot and made rapper-type arm movements all over the place. I've got it more under control these days, but I still move around quite a bit when stuff happens. Turning into a girl without an operation should have sent me jigging all the way up to the roof, you'd think. But it didn't. That's what I realised as we approached the park. I wasn't jigging about at all. Hadn't so much as twitched since Angie and I traded bods.

'Angie,' I said as we went through the park gates, 'how do you…you know…feel?'

'Feel?' she said. 'Oh, wonderful. Great. It's always been my wildest dream to look like you.'

'No, I mean you don't feel kind of…jiggy?'

'Didn't I just answer that? I feel *very* Jiggy.'

I gave up.

The Councillor Snit Memorial Park is quite big and open, with trees and grass and bright things with petals and all. Parts of it, the really ancient parts, have been there since the Golden Oldies were kids. The newer parts have tennis courts and a kiddies' play area and a little café that's never open because they can't get slave labour. We went to the little café that's never open and sat on some hard iron chairs under a tree. The chairs are bolted to the ground so no one can steal them. Not only can you not steal them but you can't turn them round to face your friends, so you have to sit all in a row looking at other things, like bushes. Actually

I was quite glad of this because sitting in a straight line helped me not look at Angie. Let me tell you, it's no fun sitting next to yourself and having to look yourself in the eye. Couldn't help the odd glance though. Oh, but she was a handsome devil, even with that thing on my nose. I mentioned this so she wouldn't get self-conscious about it.

'Heck of a boil, Ange.'

'Like I need reminding,' she said.

'You won't burst it, will you? Promise you won't burst it. I mean I know it's huge and horrible and makes you look really, really gross, but it could look a million times worse if you burst it.'

'I have no intention of bursting it,' she said, all hoity-toity. 'I do not burst boils. I don't usually *get* boils, of course, but that's because my body – my real body – is well nourished.'

'Won't be by the time he's finished with it,' Pete said.

'We'd better talk,' I said.

'We are talking,' said Angie.

'I mean about the body-switch.'

'Must we?'

'Yes, if we want to become ourselves again. We

have to give the Toilet of Doom another flush.'

'Toilet of Life,' she corrected.

'Life? You call this life? Doom I said and Doom I meant.'

'Whatever. You think another flush might reverse this?'

'Worth a try. Do you remember how you flushed away all the little people?' I asked Pete.

'Sure, why?'

'Well, it wasn't till all the little people had gone down all the little pans that the big toilet with the "F for Flush" invitation came up. So obviously you have to flush the little people again to give us another go at "F for Flush". Right?'

'What's in it for me?' he said.

'What do you mean, what's in it for you? You're our mate, Three Musketeers, one for all and all for lunch.'

'This is business. Toilet business. Come on, what are you offering?'

'Will this do?' Angie said, raising one of my fists.

Pete jumped out of his chair – 'Have to catch me first!' – and scooted up the tree we sat under.

'Like that's a problem?' Angie said, and scooted up after him.

He was out of his tiny mind if he thought he could escape Angie just by climbing a tree. She's always been better at tree-climbing than us. And she was even better at it in my body for some reason. They'd both vanished into the leaves, which were shaking like crazy, and Pete was yelling like he'd just met a tree vampire, but then the leaves parted and down he came. Thludd! It wasn't a long drop but he fell awkwardly, which made him a bit slow getting up. Too slow. Angie dropped on him from above and Pete squawked like a parrot about to be stuffed, rolled on his side, pulled his knees into his chest and crossed his arms over his head half a second before she started pummelling him.

I leaned back in my bolted iron chair, smiling. The sun was out, there was a bit of a breeze, birds gargled, and one of my best friends was being beaten up by my other best friend. All I needed was a glass of something with bubbles from the café that never opened, half a dozen straws to slurp it through, and my life would be complete. I felt amazingly calm. Never felt so calm in my life. But that wasn't all. Everything looked so much brighter than usual. More interesting somehow. I don't think I ever looked at a tree or a bush before and thought, 'Hey, cool tree, cool bush.' I did today though. And the smells. The grass, the air, the things with petals. Terrific. Why hadn't I smelt them before? Was this what it was like for real girls? If so, all I can say is no wonder most of them are quieter in class and not thumping one another all the time and cheeking the teachers.

After a while Angie got fed up of pummelling someone who didn't fight back and let Pete up. They slumped back in their seats facing the bushes. Pete was puffing a bit, fiddling with his shirt.

'I've lost a button,' he said.

'Lucky that was all,' said she.

'Do you mind if I say something, Ange?' I said gently.

She glared at me. 'Depends what.'

'Well you're a bit...um...violent today.'

'Violent?'

'Yes. I mean you always had a temper, but—'

'Temper?' she said, folding my hands into fists. 'Whaddayamean *temper*?!'

'Angela,' I said, 'a warthog with a bad home-life has a better temper than you, even on your good days.'

She aimed a swipe at me for the third time in an hour.

'See?' I said.

Surprisingly, she did. And came over all sort of shocked. All the anger and aggression drained out of her.

'You're right,' she said. 'Ever since I got this miserable excuse for a body I've felt...tense. Hands keep balling up into fists and wanting to bash things. You know what it is, don't you?'

'No, what?'

'Testosterone.'

'The chocolate bar?'

'Testosterone, you prat, not Toblerone.'

'Teswotterone?' said Pete.

'Testosserone,' I told him.

'You don't have any idea what it is, do you?' Angie said. I shrugged. She looked amazed: 'Don't you two pay attention in *any* lessons?'

'Try not to,' said Pete.

'I'm talking human biology,' she said. 'I'm talking hormones.'

'I know about hormones,' I said. 'Stallone has them.'

'Stallone?'

'Yeah. Dad says that if Stallone didn't have so many hormones he wouldn't be half as vicious and mean. Drive the old mog mental, they do. You know when the hormones are buzzing because his tail shoots up like a radio aerial and suddenly he's flying up and down the room smacking walls – smack! smack! smack! – and all you can do is keep your head down. Terrifying.'

'You want to get back to testosterone?' Angie said.

'Didn't know we'd left it.'

'I'd better spell it out for you, seeing as you're so dim. Testosterone is something that—'

'You didn't spell it,' Pete said. 'You said you'd spell it out.'

Angie ground my teeth to powder and started again. 'Testosterone, in moron terms, is something males have a lot of and females don't.'

'Like football and detentions,' I said to Pete.

'Something *inside* them,' Angie said. 'Something that makes them want to fight all the time and disrupt lessons. Makes them mad for fast cars and martial arts videos. Makes them *violent*.'

'I'm not like that,' I said.

'You can be a pain in class.'

'Naturally, I'm only human, but not the other stuff. Fast cars, martial arts, violence. I was never into any of that.'

'That's because you're a wimp,' she said.

'No, no. It's my hormones. Make me jig about instead, that's all.'

'You're not jigging now,' Pete said.

'The jig seems to go with the body, and that's out on loan. Only it doesn't make you jig,' I said to Angie. 'Makes you want to slug people.'

She stood up suddenly and started pacing up and down. As she paced, her hands – my hands – kept folding into fists, and every few steps she forced them to unfold, then a few steps later they folded again.

'I can't help myself,' she said. 'Keep wanting to bash things. God, I'd love a good fight right now!'

'Keep away from me,' Pete said.

'I said *good* fight.' She stopped pacing. Stared helplessly at us. 'I think I'm turning into a psychopath.'

'You could be right,' I said. 'Much longer on my testosserstuff and who knows what sort of monster you'll turn into.'

'The Brook Farm residents'll be forming a posse to track you down and lead you away in chains,' Pete said.

'Throw you into the deepest darkest dungeon till the flesh drops off my bones,' I added.

Angie shook herself. Came over all businesslike. 'We have to re-flush the Toilet of Doom and get our bodies back! Right away!'

'That's what I was saying a while ago.'

'Yeah, well now I'm saying it, so let's get to it.'

'We don't know it'll work,' I pointed out calmly.

'No, but it's all there is. We've got to try!'

'If it doesn't we could be stuck like this,' I said, still calm. 'Then what?'

'Then one day Angie orders her first martial arts video,' Pete said, 'and you accompany her mum to the bra stall on the market.'

I stopped being calm. I leapt up. So did Angie. We raced neck-and-neck for the park gates. Got home a good twenty minutes before Pete ambled in wiping tears of joy from his eyes.

CHAPTER TEN

We stood nervously behind Pete while he called up the Toilet of Life. The door with the notice on it appeared. Angie hadn't seen this, but Pete and I knew that when you clicked the notice the door opened on the toilet with the handle, and when you clicked the handle the screenful of smaller toilets came up, with all the little people walking round them, and when you flushed all the little people...

Except that today the notice on the door didn't say 'Vacant'. It said 'Engaged'. Pete clicked it anyway.

The door didn't open.

He clicked again. Still didn't.

Angie grabbed his shoulder and hoicked him out of the chair. She took his place, clicked 'Engaged'. The door stayed shut. She clicked again. Still shut. And again. Still.

'We seem to have a teensy-weensy problem,' I said.

'Oh, you give up too easily!'

She clicked 'Engaged' another thousand times, furiously at first, less furiously, and slower and slower, as she realised she wasn't getting anywhere. Then she sat back, staring at the closed door, chewing my lip.

No one said anything for a while. Then Pete made a suggestion.

'Milo said he knows the geezer who invented it. Maybe he could put us in touch with him. The inventor of the thing's bound to know how to get the door open.'

'It's a thought,' I said.

'A very good thought,' said Pete, patting himself on the back with a ruler.

We'd never phoned the Dakin house before. If Milo's father had been someone else we might have had the number, but he wasn't so we hadn't. They were in the book, though, along with three other Dakins.

'Four Dakin households,' I said. 'Isn't one enough?'

'One more than enough,' said Pete.

'Give me your mobile,' Angie said to him.

He wasn't keen. Nobody uses Pete's mobile, even

him most of the time; he just likes to have it around. Angie snatched it from him and buttoned the number.

'What if Face-Ache answers?' I said.

'I ask for Milo, what do you think?'

But Face-Ache didn't answer.

'Hello? Milo?' Angie said into the mouthpiece. 'It's Angie.'

'Jiggy,' I said.

'Jiggy,' she said. 'Listen, Milo, question. You know that game you mentioned the other day, the Toilet of Doom?'

'Toilet of Life,' said Pete.

'Toilet of Life,' she said. 'Remember telling us about that?'

We put our ears close to the receiver so we could hear his reply.

'Funny you should mention that,' Milo said. 'I was talking to Mr...my friend who invented it...I was talking to him about it only yesterday. Well he brought it up actually, and... Hey, you haven't been fooling with it, have you?'

'We took a look out of curiosity. Couldn't get the toilet door open.'

'Oh, that'll be the glitch.'

'The glitch?'

'My friend says it's not working the way it should. It jams, then suddenly starts up again and goes rogue.'

'Rogue? What does that mean?'

'Doesn't do what it's supposed to. It started out as an ordinary game, he says, but it's proving a bit too clever for its own good. Said I'd better not mess with it till he's sorted it out. You'd better not either.'

'Us?' Angie said, scowling at me. 'No chance. Got more sense.'

'Look, Jig,' Milo said to her. 'I can't talk now. My dad's really rattling me. Know what he's doing now? Ironing his shoelaces. I don't think I can handle this any more.'

He hung up. We all looked at the receiver.

There was a pause. Then Angie and I sank to the floor to await the end of the world. Pete didn't join us. His world was still going strong. He threw himself on the bed, put his arms under his head, smiled at the ceiling.

'I can't wait for tomorrow,' he said.

'Why, what happens tomorrow?' I asked.

'School.'

'Oh. Yes. School.'

I hadn't given school a thought till now. I don't at weekends if I can help it. But I gave it one now. Quite a big one. And groaned.

'Be a laugh,' Pete said. 'For me anyway. Not so much for you two. Specially Jiggy.'

'Why specially me?'

'Well you'll be the one in the skirt.'

'Skirt?' I said. 'Whoa. No. Not me.'

'Girls have to wear skirts to school, it's the rules,' Angie said.

'Yeah, but I'm not a girl. Not really.'

'You look like one.'

'But I'm not, that's the point.'

'No, that *is* the point,' she said. 'You look like a girl so you have to dress like one. It's the way it works.'

'But even the skirt's not the best bit,' Pete said cheerfully.

'There's *more*?' I wailed.

'Oh *yes*!' he sang. 'Oh yes, yes, *yes*! What day is it tomorrow?'

93

'Monday, why?'

'What do we do Monday afternoons?'

'Monday aftern...?'

I realised. On Monday afternoons the boys play football with Mr Rice and the girls do other things with Miss Weeks. I glanced at Angie, expecting her to be as horrified as me. But she seemed to have perked up a bit.

'Football with Rice,' she mused. 'Could be veeery interesting.'

'Oh yes,' I said. 'Right. I was forgetting. Just what you've always wanted, isn't it? Free licence to kick boys where it hurts, elbow their ribs to extinction, shove their faces in the mud. But what about me? Do you realise what I'll have to *wear*?'

'Yep,' Pete said, picturing it all.

I'd probably have been pretty amused too if he'd been in my position. But he wasn't. It was me and me alone who was going to have to wear little green knickers and a shortie gym skirt.

'I'm taking tomorrow off,' I said.

'You can't,' Angie said. 'If you don't go to school they'll think it's me not going.'

'They can think what they like.'

'You're going to school tomorrow if I have to drag you by the hair and stuff you into my Games kit personally.'

'You sound like my mother,' I said. 'You *look* more like my father, but you sound like my mother.'

'Look on it as a challenge,' Pete said. 'I mean, how often do you get to do something like this?'

'Play hockey in green knickers? Hm, now that's a tough one.'

'Netball tomorrow, not hockey,' Angie said.

'Oh, happy day.'

'Anyway, this body-swap thing could have worn off by morning. Maybe we'll wake up as ourselves.'

'And maybe we won't.'

'Even if we don't, it still might not last much longer. We could be back in the right bodies before first break tomorrow.'

'Great. There we are in Science and suddenly I'm myself again – in a girl's school uniform.'

'I won't be able to sleep tonight,' Pete said. 'The way it's looking, tomorrow's going to be the highlight of my entire school career.'

There was only one thing that made life worth

living just then: the thought that I wouldn't have to do my detention tomorrow. Angie would have to do it for me. I didn't mention this. Not yet. It wasn't much, but I needed *something* to look forward to.

CHAPTER ELEVEN

Now that Angie and I were supposed to be one another we had to swap houses. And rooms. And beds. The only good thing about this for me was that Angie hates girlie stuff. I would have screamed myself to sleep if I'd had to jog to Dreamland in a frilly nightie. Still, frilly nightie or no frilly nightie, as I was turning in that night I fell to my knees and prayed to the great toilet in the sky to flush my body back to me while I slept. You may not be surprised to hear that when I woke up next morning and found for the umpteenth time that prayers don't work, I did not fling the duvet back with a hearty cheer and start hanging party balloons.

To avoid being caught doing something un-Angie by the resident Golden Oldies, I kept out of their way as much as possible. I managed to miss them altogether that morning by being slow going down. Audrey yelled that I'd be late for the last time as she and Oliver set off for work. 'I'm coming, I'm coming!' I yelled back, but hung about upstairs till the front door closed.

When I went down I wore Angie's dressing gown over her school uniform. Pete was in the kitchen stuffing himself with Chocolate Cheerios in chocolate milk with a chocolate flake crumbled on top. Pete loves chocolate, can't get enough. And I'm the one who gets spots.

'Lemme see,' he said, tugging at the front of Angie's dressing gown.

I slapped his hand. 'Get off.'

'Have to see some time.'

'Yeah, well not till I'm ready, I have to work up to this.'

By the time we left for school I'd got more used to my new outfit (in a way it was more comfortable than my usual) but I still opened the front door like I expected the world's paparazzi to be there in force.

'Don't forget this,' Pete said.

Angie's sports bag dangled from his fingers. I snatched it off him.

'Hey, what do I call you?' he said as we crossed the road.

'Call me?'

'Well I can't call you Jiggy. Not in public. Have to be Angie.'

'Call me Angie just once and you're a chalk outline on the tarmac.'

We reached the opposite pavement. I looked at my ex-house. My house is called *The Dorks* and it's my fault, but I'm not going into that here.* I paused. How could I walk up that path, ring that plastic bell, wait patiently for my parents to open up and fail to recognise me as their son?

'I'll wait here,' I said.

'Be bold!' said Pete, and lugged me up the path. He pressed the bell. 'Hair looks nice,' he said as we stood side by side on the step.

The door was opened by my mother. Dad stood behind her looking sorry for himself, hands on hips to give his armpits room to breathe.

'Hello Pete, hello Angie,' said Mum.

Pete grunted, like he does. Not me though. I speak when spoken to.

'Hello Mum, hello Dad.'

My mother's eyebrows somersaulted over the back of her head.

---

* For the full pathetic story read *The Curse of the Poltergoose*.

'Twit,' Pete said quietly.

'No,' I said hastily. 'No, I mean "Hello Peg, hello Mel".'

Mum clawed her eyebrows back and smiled.

'Mum-Dad, Peg-Mel, what does it matter? We've all known one another so long we're like one big happy family now.'

'*Happy*?' my father cried, flinging his hands at the ceiling. 'Have you seen my *armpits*?!'

'Oh, it's you two,' a cranky voice said from above.

Angie clumped down the stairs in everything that was mine, including my school uniform and hair. My school bag and games bag clumped after her. The Boil was so big and bright today you could see it from the door without focusing. When she made it to the hall, my mother kissed her on top of the head. And here's a funny thing. I hate being kissed by my mother in front of other people, but when she kissed Angie I felt a bit jealous. I mean she's my mother and she's kissing another kid. Yes, I know it was my head her lips were decorating with saliva, but I wasn't wearing it at the time so it wasn't the same, was it?

'See you later,' she said to Angie. 'Have a good day, Musketeers!'

She went into the kitchen. Dad followed her, hands on hips.

'Still each other then,' I said as we sloped down the path. Angie didn't answer. I looked at her closely, avoiding the Boil, which believe me wasn't easy. 'Angie, why are my eyes so red? What have you been doing to them? Hey, you haven't been...?'

'No I have not!' she said. 'If you must know, the free extra attachment got stuck in your *zip*!'

'Ouch,' said Pete.

'Takes a little practice,' I said.

'I don't *want* to practise!' she said, and marched off.

We caught her up. 'My room to your liking?' I asked. 'My pyjamas?'

'Your pyjamas were disgusting. Full of earth or something, went straight in the linen basket. Your sheets weren't much better. But worst of all...' She shuddered. 'Worst of all, I had to clean your *teeth*.'

'My house is your house, my teeth are your teeth.'

'With *your* toothbrush!' she added.

'So what are you complaining about? You want to clean my teeth with *your* toothbrush?'

We'd almost made it off the estate, Angie walking a few steps in front with my boiled nose in the air, when…

'Oi, you free!'

We stepped aside to let Atkins through. He thwacked Pete's ankle with one of his bags, said 'Wotcher Ange!' to me, and scooted on to catch up with Angie. 'Hi, Jig,' I heard him say. She snarled at him. Eejit peered at the Boil. 'Ya wanna do summin' abaat that, mate. Could turn sceptic.'

Angie didn't thank him for his kind advice. She gripped his scrawny neck, lifted him off the ground, and carried him along while he gasped for breath and kicked like someone who just dived into a toilet.

'PUT THAT BOY DOWN, McCUE!' roared a deep voice.

'I didn't touch him!' I cried, spinning round with my hands up.

Miss Weeks and Mr Rice, our PE teachers, jogged by, him in his stupid red tracksuit, her in her nice green one. Miss Weeks smiled, thinking

I was fooling around, and even Rice didn't look quite as mean as usual, probably because he was with her.

'If you want to sue him for assault, Atkins,' Rice said, 'we'll gladly be witnesses for the prosecution!'

Angie dropped Eejit's neck and he scampered after the happy joggers, wormed his way between them for protection, and tried to match them jog for jog. Interesting sight. Mr Rice jogs like he's king of the world instead of a very tall berk in a red tracksuit, and Miss Weeks jogs like some golden-haired princess testing her new trainers on a trampoline. Atkins, jogging between them, looked like their pet monkey in school uniform.

Angie was still a bit ahead of us, so she reached the shopping centre first. We have to go through the shopping centre to get to school. A kid with dreadlocks and a dog leaned out of the doorway of the hairdressers and shoved a magazine in her face.

'*Fat Chance!* Help the homeless! *Fat Chance!*'

'Aw, help yourself!' Angie said, and slapped the magazine out of his hand.

The *Fat Chance* seller shrank back into the doorway until she was halfway across the square. So did the dog.

I felt a worry coming on. Dangerous combination, Angie's temper and my testoblerone. I could see it now. She bursts into the staff-room during break, head-butts every teacher in sight, the Toilet of Doom thing wears off, we get our rightful bodies back, and next morning I'm standing in front of a firing squad in Assembly.

'We have to do something,' I said to Pete. 'We have to make the Toilet of Doom work and get my body back while it's still in one piece.'

'We tried,' he said. 'Door wouldn't open. Might never open again.'

I grabbed him by the shoulders, put Angie's nose against his.

'There must be a way! We have to find it!'

'Go on, Garrett, give 'er a kiss,' said Ryan, strolling by.

Pete shook me off. 'What are you trying to do to me? This'll be all round school by Registration!'

Then he threw himself at Ryan and set about proving he didn't go in for all that soppy stuff. Watching them make mincemeat of one another, I suddenly felt very lonely. Very out of things.

CHAPTER TWELVE

You know it's weird, being a girl. The teachers and most of the other kids – even the boys – talk to you differently. Sort of gentler. Doesn't seem natural if you're not used to it. But there was one person who didn't seem to want to talk to me at all. When I walked in the classroom and sat in Angie's seat at the front, Julia Frame turned her back.

'Hey Julia, how's tricks?'

'Huh!' she said.

'Now you're not still miffed about yesterday, are you? I was just kidding around, thought you'd know.'

'It was a joke?' she said, half turning.

''Course. I was all set to let you in on it and have a big laugh with you when you zonked out of there.' I pasted a big phoney smile on Angie's chops. 'You didn't think I was *serious*, did you?'

'You really didn't mean it?'

'Not a word, Jools. Not a syllable. Not even a comma.'

It did the job. Too well. She gave a great big sob of relief, threw her arms round me, and squeezed so hard I almost burst.

'What's all this?'

I looked up. Face-Ache Dakin stood over us. I ducked out of the Frame armlock. 'Practising self-defence, sir,' I said, and made some hacking moves at her neck so he'd get the idea.

'Well, in your own time, please. This is a classroom, not a gym.'

He went to his desk, told us to settle down, settle down, and started calling the register. Calling names in alphabetical order must set Dakin up for the day. He calls the boys by their last names and the girls by their first *and* last, which seems pretty sexist to me. Even calls Milo by his last name.*

'Julia Frame!' he said, when he got to her.

'Here,' she said sulkily. She was half facing the other way again.

'Now what have I done?' I whispered over her shoulder.

'You pushed me off and hacked my neck,' she whispered back.

'I had to,' I said. 'Dakin had come in, and—'

---

* Not today though. Didn't call him anything. Milo wasn't there.

'Quiet, you two.'

'Yes, sir. Dakin had come in,' I repeated, 'and he's not big on the huggy stuff. If he hadn't come in we could've hugged all day, no prob, but there you go.'

She turned to face me again. She looked like she wanted to believe me. 'Apologise then.'

I sighed. Did I have to go through this every time I opened Angie's mouth? Well, if it helped me blend into the background…

'OK, but no more bear-hugs, not in class. I'm sorry I pushed and hacked you. All right? That cover it? Now can we just sit here and enjoy Registration with our favourite teacher?'

'McCue!' said Face-Ache.

'Here!' I said.

The class stopped talking. Every eye swivelled my way.

'I said McCue, Angela, not Mint.'

'Oh yeah, right, sorry, sir, wasn't paying attention.'

'That's quite an admission for someone in my form.'

'Thanks.'

'McCue!' he said again.

This time I let Angie handle it. Then he said her name, which comes right after mine, and I answered again. Not one eyelid batted.

Most days, including Mondays, we don't have any lessons with Face-Ache after Registration, so the second it's over we head for the door. Naturally we make as much noise as we can on the way, and naturally he screams and threatens us with every step – but not today. Today when we kicked our chairs back and charged we didn't get a peep out of him.

Outside, our mob headed for the Science Lab and crashed immediately into two other classes going in different directions. No one wanted to give way, of course, which meant there were arms and elbows and bags everywhere and for a minute it looked like there was going to be a riot. But then Mr Rice's sweet little voice was heard:

'GET TO YOUR CLASSES, YOU PEOPLE, AND STOP ALL THIS NOISE!!!'

'He's quiet today,' Angie said as we went on our way.

'Rice?' I said. 'Quiet? Have you been shovelling wax into my ears?'

108

'Dakin, I mean Dakin.'

'Yeah, I noticed that,' Pete said. 'Spooky, I thought.'

'Almost a different person,' Angie said.

'Like he hired a whole new personality from the New Personality Shop,' Pete said.

'Hey,' I said.

'Hey what?' they said.

'Maybe Face-Ache's been Toilet of Dooming too.'

We stopped in our tracks, eyes like marbles.

'Well, they have a computer at home,' Angie said.

'Yeah,' Pete said, 'but to switch bodies there has to be someone else there, and Milo says they don't get visitors.'

'Maybe they didn't need visitors,' I said. 'Maybe *they* switched.'

'Are you saying it wasn't Dakin the Father taking Registration but Dakin the *Son*?' Angie said.

'It would explain why Milo wasn't in class.'

'No. Couldn't happen. If Dakin woke up and discovered he'd turned into Milo overnight he'd have a heart attack.'

'That's it!' (This was Pete in case you wonder.) 'Face-Ache has a heart attack and Milo leaves him twitching on the floor. "Free at last!" he thinks, sprinting for school in his father's body.'

Angie shook her head. 'Milo's a young kid in the prime of life and his dad's a dried-up old stick insect. If you were Milo, would you leap at the chance to wear a bag of bones like that?'

'Besides,' I said, 'if Milo took Registration there'd be tell-tale signs. Milo signs. We'd have spotted them.'

'Don't look round,' said Pete. 'I think we're being followed.'

Angie and I looked round. By this time we were the last of our class in the corridor. Last but one. Julia was still there. Trailing after us. After me.

'Think you've got yourself a fan,' Angie said.

'Only because she thinks I'm you.'

'No. Because you're being nice to her. Nicer than I ever was.'

It was during morning break that Angie and I had to use the wrong school toilets for the first time. We'd put it off as long as possible, but couldn't hold it in any longer. We were standing in the corridor between the Boys and the Girls. No one had gone in or come out of either of them for a while but we still hung back. It's a big thing, using the opposite team's toilets.

'Go on then,' Angie said.

'After you,' I said.

'What's the big deal? All cubicles, the Girls. No one'll see.'

'There are cubicles in the Boys too.'

'Be bold, Jig,' said Pete.

'Will you stop saying that?' I said.

'And don't hang about in there,' said Angie, shoving me at the Girls.

'Hang about? This'll be the fastest pee in history.'

I was about to go in when Mr Heathcliff arrived. Heathcliff is the school caretaker, and the most depressing person you ever met. He lives in a cupboard full of brooms and buckets and stuff, and he's always shuffling on to the scene muttering things you can't make out. Like today. As he shuffled round the corner he paused, looked me up and down – me with my hand on the door of the Girls – as if to say he knew all about me and was thinking of selling the story to the tabloids and doing interviews.

'Morning, Mr Heathcliff,' I said.

'Er-*rum*!' said Heathcliff, which is all he ever seems to say, and shuffled off.

I threw the holy door back and shot in. A girl's gotta do what a girl's gotta do, even when she isn't one. I ran into a cubicle, bolted the door, dropped the fire-damaged underpants, and...well you know the rest. Twenty seconds later I was washing Angie's hands and checking her hair in the mirror. Then I went out – and collided with four girls coming in.

'You were supposed to stop people,' I said to Pete and Angie.

'We tried,' said Pete. 'We failed.'

I let it go. It was Angie's turn.

'No one comes in,' she said. 'But *no* one. Right?'

She went into the Boys. Pete and I stood to attention outside. And of course a batch of boys came along right away. One of them was my arch-enemy Bryan Ryan. Only today he didn't know he was my arch-enemy.

'What's up, Minty?' he said when I blocked his way.

'Can't go in.'

'Why not?'

'Teachers' orders. Flooded. Have to use the Girls.'

'You're kidding.'

'Would I kid you, Bry-Ry?'

'Well what do the girls use?'

'The Teachers.'

'So what do the teachers use?'

'The Boys.'

'Oh.'

They went into the Girls. Pete and I legged it round the corner. We heard the screams and yells. Peeked out just in time to see Ryan and his pals shoot out again, ducking flying toilet rolls.

CHAPTER THIRTEEN

Take it from me, the hardest part about being a girl at school isn't the lessons, it's remembering to sit with your legs together all the time. But even this was nothing compared to Games that Monday afternoon. Things looked like getting kind of tricky before we even left the changing room. I didn't know where to look when the girls started to get into their togs, so I glued my eyes to the ceiling. They thought I was playing the fool. Thought I was playing it even more when I put my Games knickers on. Games knickers are worn over ordinary knickers. But I wasn't wearing ordinary knickers. I was wearing fire-damaged Y-fronts.

There was one last thing to put on when we were all kitted out in our sporty skirts and knickers. A bib. Yes, a bib. I never knew they were called that till then. Angie had kept it pretty quiet and I don't blame her.

'Why are they called bibs, miss?' I asked. 'I mean what do you think we're going to do, dribble custard suddenly?'

'Very funny, Angela.'

Miss hadn't got changed in the same room as us, of course, but she wore the same natty little green outfit – except for the bib. Probably felt she'd got the dribble under control by the age of almost thirty. As we filed out, I noticed Julia Frame trying to get near me and shoved Jodie Duthie and Jodie Gold between us.

The football pitch is over to the right as you go down from the changing rooms. The boys were swarming towards it, yelling, rolling over, belting one another, while we girls walked to the netball court in a quiet, orderly fashion. I always wondered how the girls manage this and I wasn't any the wiser now. I don't think I ever felt so stupid in my life. I mean I might have looked like a girl, but I wasn't, not really, not inside. In my head I was a boy in a short dress, knickers and bib. Someone wolf-whistled from the football pitch. I didn't need to look to know who.

The netball court has a high wire fence all round

115

it, like a big cage. Miss Weeks opened the gate and we trooped in. Then she stuck her arms out like a scarecrow.

'Red team that end, blue team that!'

'Which am I, miss?' I asked.

'Look at your chest, Angela.'

'Why, what's wrong with it?'

'Your bib, don't be silly.'

I looked at the bib on Angie's chest. It was a red one (bib, not chest). About half the girls wore red bibs, the rest wore blue ones. Some of the red girls were going one way and some of the blues were going the other, while a few of each stayed where they were, in the middle. I thought I'd better stick to the middle too and hope for the best. I gazed through the wire fence. Felt like a prisoner in there. I was, in a way. Over on the football pitch some of the boys were banging balls about and tripping one another up and Mr Rice was screaming, 'Hegarty, Sprinz, stop fighting!' For the first time ever I wished I was over there with them, about to play football.

Something large and shapeless climbed into the corner of my eye. Julia Frame. I was starting to understand what Angie had against her. I ran across the court to get as far away from her as possible. I glanced back. She wasn't following.

'What are you doing over there, Angela?' Miss Weeks shouted. 'In position, please.'

'I have a position?' I shouted back.

She didn't answer, just threw another arm out. I followed the arm until I came to Megan Larkin.

'Megan, what's my position? Must have got sunstroke yesterday. Can't remember things. Like how to play netball.'

She frowned. Megan does a lot of frowning when I'm around, though usually when I'm in my own body. She's always telling me to grow up and stuff.

'Sunstroke?' she said. 'It wasn't that sunny yesterday.'

'It wasn't? Well I said I don't remember things. Where do I go?'

'Look at your bib.'

I glanced at Angie's chest again. 'Looking.'

'It says "GS". That means you're goal shooter.'

'Cool. So what do I do exactly?'

She peered at me suspiciously. 'What are you up to, Angie?'

'Up to? Me? Come on, Meg, help me out here, help me out.'

'You stand near the net. That net. You throw the ball into it.'

'Thanks. Buy you a glass of water some time.'

I sauntered towards my net. While I was walking I heard Rice yelling orders over on the footie pitch.

'Divide yourselves into two teams by your last initial!' he hollered. '"As" to "Ms" this side of the line, "Ns" to "Zs" that side! Come on, move it, move it!'

A few boys ambled over the line one way or the other, but the rest just stood there scratching their heads.

'What do you mean last initial, sir?'

It was Pete. I frowned. It should have been me over there annoying Mr Rice. Annoying Mr Rice is one of those things I do really well.

'What do I mean?!' Rice bawled. 'I mean the first letter of your last name, boy, what *else* could I mean?!'

'Oh, right.' Pete glanced my way, then said, in a specially loud voice so I wouldn't miss it: 'So if my name was, say, *McCue*, my initial would be "M", right? It wouldn't be, say, "B" for Big Girl's Blouse?'

I leapt at the fence, fingers like claws through the holes. 'I'll get you for that, Garrett, you snot-eyed relic!'

Just then I heard a voice in the distance. My voice.

'It's all right, Jig! I mean Angie! I'll do it!'

I dropped off the fence as Angie, in my body and footie gear, put my head down and started towards Pete like a blind bull. Pete saw her coming, spun round, headed for the edge of the pitch.

'Garrett, where are you going?!' Rice bawled.

Pete didn't answer. Or stop. Rice tried a different approach.

'Set one boot off this pitch and you'll be cleaning the mud off mine for the rest of term!'

Pete swerved. If there's one thing he hates, it's cleaning things. You just have to look at his feet to know that. He made a right angle at the edge of the pitch and started along another side. Not very bright. All Angie had to do now was change direction and take a short cut.

'And what do you think *you're* up to, McCue?!' Rice screamed.

'Gonna duff up Garrett!' Angie yelled.

'Oh no you're not!' he bellowed, going after her. 'There will be no duffing-up in my lesson unless I am the duffer!'

'You are, you are!' hooted several boys at once.

This was followed by a mighty roar as Angie made a flying leap, folded my arms round Pete's legs, and pitched him face-to-face with the worms. Then she jumped up, threw herself astride his back, and grabbed his hair. I don't know what she planned to do next because Rice got there too soon and hauled her off. But he wasn't purple with rage like he usually is when catching a kid pulping another kid. Not a bit of it.

'That was some tackle, McCue! Perhaps you have hidden talents! Let's double check, shall we? Ryan!!!'

Ryan ran up. Ryan will do anything to please Rice, the creep, mainly because football is the only lesson he's any good at.

'Sir?'

'Run up to my office and fetch a rugger ball!'

'Rubber ball?' said Bry-Ry.

'Rugger ball, *rugger*, and be quick about it!'

'But why do you want a rugger ball, sir? We're playing football.'

'Change of plan! McCue just made the best tackle I've seen from a boy in years! I want to find out if he can do it again! Speed o' light, lad, speed o' light! Everyone else, switch pitch!'

Ryan scowled – he's dotty about football, not rugby – and headed for the changing rooms, while Mr Rice marched towards the rugby pitch. The boys watched him go. When he got there Rice turned, saw that he was alone, and gently asked the boys to please be kind enough to join him.

'GETYERBACKSIDESOVEREREYAUSELESS BUNCHALAY-ABOUTS!'

'All set, Angela?'

I looked round. 'Do you mind if I just watch today, miss? Think I've twisted my ankle.'

I limped bravely round in a little circle to prove it.

'You weren't limping just now.'

'Trying not to, I hate missing netball, but it's so painful.'

'Just do your best. Right, girls, let's get cracking!'

So I played netball for the first time in my life.

I picked it up as I went along, made a lot of mistakes while picking, but after a while I started to get the hang of it. And guess what? I was good at it. No. Better than good. I was a natural. Perhaps it was Angie's body, but even without my jigginess I was so nippy on her feet that the world was a blur. When the ball came my way, all I had to do was reach out and I was holding it. Then all I had to do was stand on tiptoe, make a sharp upward movement with my borrowed elbows, and the ball was dropping out the bottom of the net and my team was cheering and Miss Weeks was saying, 'Oh well done, Angela, well done, my you *have* come on suddenly!'

Yes, at last I'd found a sport I could do. And one I quite enjoyed. But talk about Sod's Law. Have you heard of Sod's Law? Sod was this ancient Scottish saint who wrong things kept happening to. Whenever Saint Sod prayed for stuff to happen it didn't, and whenever he prayed that it wouldn't it did. This became known as Sod's Law, and it works pretty well for people who aren't saints too, especially if their name's McCue. Like until that day I'd never given netball a thought, and suddenly I discover that netball and me are made for one another. The Sod's Law part was that the only way I'd be able to play it was if I stayed a girl.

Every now and then while I was being brilliant at netting balls I glanced across at the rugby field to see how they were getting on. There was one kid who looked like he wanted to make a name for himself. He did a lot of weaving in and out with his head down, this kid, the ball pinned to his chest. A lot of elbowing and shouldering people who got in the way and a lot of flying through the air and grabbing legs so the owners nose-dived into the daisies. After a while anyone who had any sense headed the other way when he came near. I would have done, too, if I'd been there. He was terrifying. And who was this warrior of the weird-shaped ball?

That's right. Angie. Pretending to be me and shattering my carefully-built-up reputation as an utterly useless sportsman. Spoiling everything.

CHAPTER FOURTEEN

If you're a boy at Ranting Lane you have to strip off after Games and get in the showers with all the other boys. I hate that, but I would have hated it even more if I'd had to shower with the girls. Fortunately the girls don't have to take showers if they don't want to, so I just got dressed again with my eyes on the ceiling, wishing girls wouldn't keep coming up to me in towels and patting me on the back, saying things like 'Hey Angie, didn't know you were such a wiz at netball, can I be in your team next time?' Julia kept looking at me with pride, like she'd coached me personally or something. I gave her the royal wave a couple of times, then cut her out of my will.

I wondered how Angie was getting on. Mr Rice never lets anyone off showers unless they have a fake doctor's note, like Pete, so she would have to shower with the boys. Or so I thought. Should have learnt by now never to underestimate old Ange.

I waited for her and Pete to come out of the changing room. Pete had mopped most of the dirt off his face, but Angie hadn't bothered. There was mud in my hair, my ears, on my face and neck, under my nails, you name it, there was mud there. Even the Boil was all muddy, though I was glad to see she'd managed not to burst it. I asked her how she'd got out of showers.

'Told Rice I had a rash someplace private,' she said.

'That wouldn't stop him throwing a kid in to drown.'

'Ah, but Angie's flavour of the day,' Pete said. 'You never saw the old Ricebag so pleased. Says she's a real find. As a rugby player.'

I turned away to hide my misery. Because of what Angie had done today, Rice would expect the same sort of performance from me when I got my body back. My only consolation was that next time she donned the little green knickers and bib, Angie would also find herself the star of a sport she hates.

Games is the last lesson on Monday so we headed for the gates with everyone else. But then I remembered.

'Whoa! Back up. Detention! Dakin!'

'Curses, forgot that,' said Pete.

'Ah well, can't be helped. See you later.'

'Where are you going?' Angie said.

'Home. To the wrong house. Garrett and McCue have detentions, not Angie Mint.'

'What? Oh no!'

'Better clean yourself up though. Face-Ache won't be all that thrilled when you turn up looking like that.'

'So what's he gonna do,' she said furiously, 'tell me to go *home*?'

She stormed back into school. Pete followed. It's the first time I've ever seen him head for detention laughing.

When I reached the estate I found something happening in the street between our houses. Barriers had been put up round a man pickaxing a hole while three others watched.

'Buried treasure?' I said. They didn't seem amused.

I went indoors and straight up to Pete's room. I turned on his PC, called up the Toilet of Life with a beating heart. The door with the notice appeared.

It still read 'Engaged'. I clicked about insanely for a while, hoping enough clicks would wear it down, force it to get vacant, but it didn't work.

Later, when Pete came in, he had some news.

'You'll never guess. Milo's disappeared. Dakin said his bed wasn't slept in last night. He must have gone out after we phoned and not come back.'

'Wow.'

'I've never seen Face-Ache like that,' he said. 'All nervy, not strict at all. Didn't even set us any work, just talked.'

'About Milo?'

'No, about the women's darts championships in Outer Mongolia. Of course about Milo.'

'So what did he say?'

'Dunno, wasn't really listening. There was this spider dangling from the ceiling right over his head and I wanted to see if it would land.'

'And that's all?'

'Yeah. Didn't land.'

'I mean that's all you heard him say about Milo, that he didn't come home last night?'

'Just about. He asked us if he'd said anything before he scarpered.'

'What did you tell him?'

'Nothing. What's to tell? He said if Milo isn't home by teatime he's going to the police.'

'This isn't good,' I said.

'Depends what he's got in for tea. Jig, think about it. There could be a house-to-house search. Doors kicked in. Tracker dogs up the stairs. We could be thrown into chairs and blinded by spotlights, everything we say taken down and used against us.' His eyes lit up. 'Hey, if Milo's found in a ditch we might even be on the *telly*.'

I shook my head at him. 'I just don't believe you sometimes.'

'Yeah,' he said, eyes still lit, 'but the *telly*...'

CHAPTER FIFTEEN

For tea that day, Angie's favourite was put in front of me. Spinach lasagne. I'm not a big fan of lasagne even when it doesn't look like cat sick. I pushed it round and round the plate, hoping it would drop over the side and burn a hole through the table.

'What's wrong with it?' Audrey asked.

'You tell me,' I said.

'What a waste. I paid good money for that. You eat too much when you come in from school, I'm always telling you.'

It was like being at home. Only the names had been changed. And the faces. And furniture.

After tea – after I'd washed up (it was Angie's turn on their rotten rota) – Pete and I left the house. The hole was still in the road. The man who'd been digging it, and the three men who hadn't, sat together in the front of their van. Digging Man was tucking into a pizza he'd just had delivered. The other three were watching. Must have been trainees.

'Remember you have different parents now,' Pete said as we approached *The Dorks*.

'After that lasagne how could I forget?' I said.

Once again my mum opened the door. She's usually quickest off the mark when the bell goes. She didn't look in the best of moods.

'Hi, Peg.' I was getting good at this. 'Jiggy in?'

'In his room. Go on up.'

'Thanks, Mum.'

We went upstairs.

'Don't you knock?' Angie said as we barged in.

'Since when do I have to knock on my own door?' I said.

'That door is no longer yours. Keep checking the mirror, you'll get it eventually.'

It was then that I realised there was something different about the place. Something very different.

'Angie, what…what have you done?'

'I tidied things up.'

'Tidied things up? It's like I was never here. Never put my personal stamp on it.'

'Yes, it's quite an improvement,' she said.

'And what are all these cushions doing?'

'They're cushions, what do you want them to do?'

'I mean what are they doing here? And so many. Are you breeding them or something?'

They were everywhere you looked, about three thousand of them.

'I like cushions,' she said.

'If you like them so much why are there only two in your room? Your real room across the road. Where you sleep. Where you *belong*.'

'We don't have a cushion surplus. Stacks here though. Your mum likes cushions too. Says you and your dad are always taking the mickey out of her and her cushions, so she buys them and puts them away for a rainy day.'

'Cushions won't keep much rain off,' Pete said, stretching his arms out and belly-flopping on to a pile of them.

'Apart from the big cushion invasion,' I said, trying not to look at them, 'what's new at *The Dorks*?'

'Well, your mother's not speaking to your dad,' Angie said.

'So what's new at *The Dorks*?'

'Oh but this is really heavy. She's furious about him taking Stallone to the vet's behind her back.'

'Why does she have a vet behind her back?' Pete said from the cushions.

'You mean he actually went through with it?' I said to Angie. 'I thought it was just a heat-of-the-moment threat and he'd get over it.'

'No. He took the morning off work specially. Told me everything while hiding from your mum. How he put on these extra-thick Help the Aged lumberjack gloves and snuck up on Stallone while he was eating the jellied pigeon brains he'd bought to distract him. How he put a rope round his neck and dragged him squealing into the dead-budgie cage.'

'Stallone's too big to go through the door of the dead-budgie cage,' I said.

'Your dad was up half the night turning one side into a flap. With a catch.'

'And it held? Amazing. Whatever he's good at it isn't DIY. Well, well. So he had the mad mog done, did he? Poor old Stallone. How's he taking it?'

'He's not. He broke out of the cage in the waiting room. Hasn't been seen since.'

'Like Milo,' said Pete.

'Milo wasn't about to be snipped,' I reminded him.

'We don't know that.'

Angie said: 'Maybe we ought to go and look for him.'

'Who, Milo or Stallone?'

'I meant Stallone, but we could make it a double search. Soon as we've checked if the Toilet of Doom's still engaged.'

'It is,' I said. 'I took a look while you two were in detention.'

'That was then,' she said. 'From what Milo said there's no telling when it'll work next, so we're going to check it again.'

We yanked Pete out of the cushions and went downstairs. We left the house, started across the road.

'Stallone!' I cried suddenly.

'It's no good shouting for him,' Angie said.

'No, I've just seen him. Look!'

He sat under a lamp-post some way along, one leg in the air. He'd been licking this leg when I shouted his name and it was still up there, drying out, when we started towards him. It wasn't till we got within hissing distance that he lowered the leg

133

and ran round the corner on it and three others.

'Scaredy cat,' said Pete.

'I wonder why he's still hanging about if he's left home?' Angie said.

'Nowhere else to go,' I said.

'Maybe we should go after him.'

'We'd never catch him. He'll come home when he's ready. Or not.'

We turned back. The four workmen were at their hole again. As we drew near there was a great roar and the man who'd been doing the pickaxing and pizza-eating started shaking himself silly with one of those big deafening road drills. The other three wore earmuffs and watched.

Pete's room overlooks the street, so the drill was still pretty loud up there, even with the window closed. Angie pushed him into his swivel chair and told him to call up the Toilet of Doom. He did. And this time...

'Told you it was worth trying,' Angie said.

'Click it, Pete, click it,' I said excitedly.

Pete clicked the 'Vacant' sign and the door swung open. And there it was, with the graffiti on the wall behind it.

The Toilet of Life
A Manx Game

'What now?' Angie said.

'He clicks the little handle on the side,' I told her. 'Go on, Pete, click the handle before it freezes again.'

'I was going to.'

He clicked the little handle. It moved, there was a flushing sound, and the toilet was immediately replaced by the screenful of much smaller toilets and little walking people.

'Get flushing!' I said.

'Will you stop giving me orders?' he said as one of the little toilet seats flew up. A little person gave a yelp and dived in, legs wriggling. There was a small flush and he slithered all the way down.

Angie and I looked at one another with each other's shining eyes. It was going to happen! We were in with a chance of getting our bodies back!

Pete set to work. Soon little people were yelping and diving and getting flushed all over the screen.

And then they were gone. All of them. The screen changed. And we were looking at the Toilet of Life itself, and the immortal words:

Feel that your life has gone down the pan?
Well here's your chance to swap it
for a better one.
Just invite someone round who's really got
it made and hit 'F for Flush'!

Angie and I slapped hands in the air.

At the very instant we slapped hands the drill out in the street stopped. It stopped because the workman and his watchers had drilled through a power cable. All the electricity on our side of the estate went off. Pete's screen went blank.

And stayed that way till way past bedtime.

CHAPTER SIXTEEN

First thing in the morning I went to Pete's room and activated his computer. He raised his bleary head from the pillow.

'What are you doing?'

'Checking the T of D's still vacant.'

It was. But there was no point going to the next stage because Angie wasn't there. She had to be there when we hit 'F for Flush' or I might find I'd swapped her body for something even worse, like a cockroach.

We'd arranged to meet for school half an hour earlier that morning. We hadn't had a chance to look for Milo last night and wanted to see if he'd returned home. The street was quiet when Pete and I left the house. The electricity vandal and his watchers hadn't arrived yet for another bash at their hole. Angie came out of *The Dorks* as we reached it. The Boil was starting to fester. Looked like it was getting all set to blow. I put Pete between us.

On the way to Milo's, Angie updated me on life at home. Mum still wasn't talking to Dad because Stallone was still missing.

'She sent your dad out to look for him last night. He was gone for hours, no sign. Peg says he'll be doing the same thing tonight and every night until Stallone's found either purring at the top of his voice or pulped by a juggernaut.'

When we got to Pizzle End Road we lurked behind a tree near Milo's and waited for someone to come out. The only one who did was Face-Ache. They never go to school together, so this told us nothing. His walk did though. All stooped and tragic like he was really suffering. Still, we had to make sure. When Dakin was well on his way we opened the gate and rapped the super-shiny brass knocker for a couple of minutes. Nothing rapped back.

'Tracker dogs,' said Pete as we left.

'Where?' I said.

He rubbed his hands together. 'Any time now.'

We were approaching Mr Mann's bus shelter and the luxury apartment building opposite. Men in white gloves and smart dungarees were carrying brand new furniture in from a removal van.*

---

* Into the luxury apartment building, not the bus shelter.

'My dad gets really worked up about that place,' Pete said, meaning the luxury apartment building. 'Gets right up his snout that some people have that sort of money while he only has one car, six ties and a biro.'

'Wonder who owns them?' I said.

'My dad,' said Pete.

'No, no, the flats. The building.'

'No one knows,' Angie said. 'The owner's anonymous.'

'I know that. What I'm saying is, why would someone who owns a block of flats keep it secret?'

'Some tax dodge maybe, who knows, who cares?'

'What's going on there?' said Pete.

Four big teenage boys stood over Mr Mann, who'd just looked up from his paper to see what was in his light. One of the boys was Jolyon Atkins, Eejit Atkins's older brother. We keep out of Jolyon's way. Everyone keeps out of Jolyon's way. He has this barbed-wire tattoo round his neck and the four fingers of his left hand are tattooed with H.A.T.E. Morons who have H.A.T.E. tattooed on one hand usually have L.O.V.E. tattooed on the other. Not Jolyon. He has H.A.T.E. on both.

We crept closer to catch what Jolyon and his gang were saying to Mr Mann. It went something like this:

'You's a tramp, 'at's wot you are.'

'Yer. Why'n't you tramp orf to sum uvver place?'

'Yer. We don' want your kind 'ere.'

'Nah. You're scum. Sod orf.'

'Yer. Or we'll fump ya.'

'Give yer 'ell.'

'Yer.'

Mr Mann took his glasses off, smiled, and said, 'Take a seat, lads, sit and chat awhile. You're welcome to share my paper. Tell me, what do you make of the latest from the Balkans?'

Jolyon's forehead slumped over his eyes. It was only a little forehead so it didn't have far to go.

'You takin' the proverbial?'

Mr Mann frowned kindly up at him. 'Sorry? Proverbial what?'

Jolyon growled. 'You fink I'm fick, dunyou?'

'No, not at all. Here, let's read the Obituaries together.'

Jolyon gripped Mr Mann by the lapel of his old overcoat. The other three leered, made sandpapery noises with their tonsils, all set to enjoy themselves as Jolyon's spare hand folded and drew back.

But then: 'Atkins, you lame-brained twonk, put that tramp down!'

It was my voice. My real voice. And it wasn't coming from me.

'What do you say we keep out of this?' I said to Angie out of the side of my mouth. 'I'd kind of like that body to live to see another…'

But she was already stalking towards the bus shelter, where the bundle of bullet-heads stood gaping at her in amazement.

'Wot joo call me, McCue?' Jolyon said.

'Lame-brained twonk,' Angie said. 'And I was being polite.'

'He'll tear her to shreds!' I said to Pete. 'Tear *my body* to shreds!'

'Don't worry,' Pete said, 'you won't feel a thing.'

Now she was standing in front of Jolyon, glaring up at him. She was quite a bit smaller than him, even in my body, but she didn't seem afraid. Well, why should she? By the time she came round, the broken legs, cauliflower ears and black eyes would probably be back on me. While glaring up at Jolyon she unlocked his fingers from the tramp's lapel. Mr Mann just sat there looking quietly amused.

'Joo know oo yaw messin' wiv?' Jolyon said.

''Course,' Angie replied. 'I'm messin' wiv a cretin. A twerp. Jolyon Atkins, who has a prune for a brain.'

I gulped. 'No,' I whispered. 'Take it back, Ange, take it back.'

She didn't take it back, and Jolyon's forehead dropped even further. Then he gave her a shove. On the shoulder. It was meant to be the first of many shoves and lots of other stuff besides. I knew it, Pete knew it, Jolyon's Merry Men knew it, even Mr Mann probably knew it. The only one who didn't seem to was Angie.

'Do that again and you'll make me angry,' she said to Jolyon. 'You wouldn't like me when I'm angry, Atkins.'

And of course Jolyon did it again. Other shoulder this time. His cronies chuckled. This was gonna be soooo funny. They were still chuckling when a fist shot out and dotted Jolyon on the nose. It must have been quite a dot because Jolyon said something like 'Uh?' and immediately sat down.

He stared up at Angie in surprise for a few seconds, then his eyelids fell and his head slumped forward. And that was that.

The chuckling of the cronies stopped. Angie turned to them. 'Anyone else?' They held their hands up, shook their heads. 'Well get him out of here, he makes this bus shelter look untidy.'

Jolyon's slack-jawed chums slotted their mitts into his pits and dragged him off, face down, the toes of his shoes scraping the pavement.

'Come on, Pete!' I said.

We reached the bus shelter three seconds later, panting for breath.

'You all right, Ange?' I asked. 'It was all so quick, couldn't get here before! Did they hurt you? You want us to go after them and give 'em what for? Just say the word, Ange!'

'It's all right, everything's under control,' she said quietly.

And then it all floated through my mind: the not-so-distant day when I'm back in my own body and Jolyon Atkins remembers what happened here today and comes looking for me with a sledgehammer.

I heard Mr Mann's voice in the distance. 'What's your name, son?'

I heard the reply. 'Angie. I mean Jiggy. Jiggy McCue. This is Angie.'

I felt a jab in the ribs. I nodded to back her up. 'Yes, that's right.'

'Well, Jiggy McCue,' he said to her, 'I'm not sure how I would have come out of that little encounter if you hadn't come along, but I'm in your debt. I'd like to give you something for your trouble, a reward of some sort.' He paused, then spread his arms to take in all his worldly goods. 'I'd *like* to, but as you see…'

'Forget it,' Angie said. 'Glad to be of help.'

'Very kind of you,' Mr Mann said. 'But if there's anything I can ever do for you, all you have to do is ask.'

'Thanks.' She turned to go. Then turned back. 'Wait. There might be something. A friend of ours has gone missing. Milo Dakin, lives just up the road there.'

'I know Milo,' Mr Mann said. 'Good boy. Often stops for a few words.'

'Yes, well he didn't go home on Sunday night

and he wasn't at school yesterday. 'Course, he might turn up today, but if he doesn't...'

'You sound concerned.'

'I am. We all are. Things haven't been all that great at home lately.'

'It's just him and his dad these days,' I said. 'And Mr Dakin's pretty strict.'

'He's a fanatic,' Pete said. 'We should know, he's our form tutor.'

'So I was just wondering if you've seen him,' Angie said.

Mr Mann sucked his lip for a while, deep in thought and hair. Then he said: 'I can tell you something. It's not much, but you must promise not to pass it on to a living soul.'

I looked at the others. 'You have our word.'

'Well then, you may rest assured that Milo is safe and has a roof over his head.'

'Has he told you that?' Angie said.

Mr Mann looked away. 'One hears things on the street.'

'But you know where he is?'

'I can say no more. I won't break a confidence.'

'But think of his dad,' I said. 'He's worried sick.'

At this he threw his head back and his great thick mane flew about his shoulders. A tiny lodger left his beard in a hurry.

'From what I've heard, a little worry wouldn't do that gentleman any harm. Might make him realise what he could lose if he doesn't start behaving more like a father, less like Franco.'

'The hairdresser?' said Pete.

'The dictator. Now what happened to my paper...?'

His paper had fallen on the ground. I scooped it up and handed it to him. He gave a bristly smile. His teeth looked like they hadn't been cleaned since the middle of the last century.

'I'd be lost without my morning paper. Mr Murdoch the newsagent very kindly brings it to me every morning – free of charge.'

'You must know it by heart,' Pete said.

We went on to school.

CHAPTER SEVENTEEN

The first thing we saw after fighting our way through the school gates was a big notice on a board. Standing beside the board was our depressed caretaker, Mr Heathcliff.

'Morning, Mr Heathcliff,' I said.

'Er-*rum*,' he said, and pointed at the notice.

The notice said that all pupils must go to the main hall right after Registration, or else. No hints what for, so there were a few worried looks. We only go to the main hall once a week, for Assembly, and Assembly wasn't today. It could mean anything.

'Thanks a lot, Mr Heathcliff,' I said as the bell went.

'Er-*rum*.'

'I don't know why you bother to talk to that miserable specimen,' Pete said on the way to class.

'Oh, I enjoy our little chats,' I said.

Not only was Milo not in class again, but his old

man wasn't either. Miss Weeks was waiting for us instead.

'Where's Face-Ache, miss?' Pete asked.

'Who?'

'Dakin. Mister. Where?'

'Mr Dakin's about. You'll see him shortly.'

'Oh goody.'

When she called the register she missed Milo completely. It was as if he'd ceased to exist. The moment she finished – even before we could kick our chairs over and race for the door – she stood up and smiled.

'Neil Downey, come to the front please.'

'Who me, miss?'

'Yes Neil, you. The rest of you stay seated.'

Downey slouched to the front, where Miss Weeks turned his shoulders round to face the class.

'The register informs me that it's Neil's birthday today. How about "Happy Birthday to You", everyone?'

'Happy birthday to you,' we mumbled, and piled out. Downey isn't the most popular kid in the galaxy.

We joined the happy throng in the corridor and set off for the hall. Most of the school was there already, muttering quietly. There was a row of chairs on the stage, with teachers on them looking serious – including Dakin, who looked even tenser than usual.

'Worry,' Angie said. 'Maybe he's human after all.'

'Maybe pigs have wheels,' Pete said.

'Wings,' I said.

'What?' he said.

'Pigs have wings,' I said.

'Do they?' he said.

'No,' I said.

'So why tell me they have?'

When the rest of the school had come in and sat down, Mr Hubbard our headteacher came on with a policeman and a policewoman.

'Double strippergram for Downey's birthday?' Pete said.

But it wasn't a double strippergram. Mother Hubbard introduced the couple in blue and then they took it in turns, like they'd been rehearsing all night, to tell us about Milo's disappearance and ask us to come forward if we had any information or thoughts as to his whereabouts.

And that was it. We filed out again.

'What do we do?' I said.

'About what?' said Pete.

'Well, Mr Mann seems to know where Milo is. We ought to tell.'

'Can't,' said Angie. 'You gave him our word.'

'Yeah, but this is serious. We could be had up for withholding stuff. Criminal offence.'

'They cut your hands off for that in Greece,' Pete said.

'Greece?' I said.

'Well, somewhere.'

'Also,' Angie said, 'if we shop Mr Mann and they interrogate him and he tells everything he knows and they find Milo, they'll ask Milo why he left home, and it might come out that he has a lousy father, which could land Face-Ache in pretty hot water, maybe even lose him his job.'

'That's true,' said Pete.

He was halfway to the head's office before we caught him and hauled him back.

First lesson of the day was Geography. Our Geography teacher, Mrs Porterhouse, is very tiny and twice as skinny, with a voice like a bread knife. She isn't too bad most of the time, but every so often she does something she thinks will make Geography more interesting. Some things are OK, like the field trips – trips to fields – but most are as boring as the back of Bryan Ryan's head. Recently Mrs P had been failing to get us interested in the people and customs of other lands, what they eat, what sort of houses and huts they live in, things like that. Not exactly stirring stuff, but at least you could sleep through it. No dozing today though. Today the mad old bat was going to show us how they dance in Argentina. She was going to show us the tango. And make us dance it. With one another.

'Miss,' I said as she led us into the gym where the sacrifice was to take place, 'why don't we leave the Argentininians to do their own stupid dance and sit down quietly and look at their stamps instead?'

No dice. She slipped a CD into the little machine she'd brought with her.

'Now pay attention, everyone. The tango is a slow ballroom dance that...' The music started before she was ready. 'Well, watch me.' She started gliding and jerking round the gym like a grasshopper with a wooden leg. 'You see? Looong gliding movements punctuated by ab-*rupt* pauses. Looong gliding movements punctuated by...'

It wouldn't have been quite so bad if we'd had to spend the lesson watching her make a fool of herself, but she wanted us to make fools of ourselves too. Pete realised how it was going to work even before I did and grabbed the nearest girl so he wouldn't get stuck with me. Kelly Ironmonger screamed and beat him off.

Pete held his hands out. 'Anybody?'

There were no takers, but the Porterhouse took charge.

'Susan, he's all yours.'

Susan Berry's face screwed up like an old sweet wrapper. 'Dance with Garrett? Oh *Miss*!'

'He's no worse than the rest. And at least he's keen, unlike some.'

'Some' meant every other boy there, who'd suddenly discovered their fingernails, the ceiling, the floor, and how not to whistle.

I caught Angie looking at me. When she saw that she'd got my full attention she gave me a cruel grin and skipped across the gym – yes, skipped, in *my* body! – and grabbed Laura Porritt by the hand.

Laura tried to yank it back but Angie was too strong today and pulled her to her, body to body, face to face. Then she did a looong glide followed by an abrupt halt. Laura wailed miserably, but Angie kept her grip and did the same thing again, looong glide, abrupt halt, while Mrs Porterhouse clapped. Yes clapped, silly woman.

'Well done, Jiggy, you've really got a feel for the tango!'

I turned to the wall and banged Angie's head slowly against it. In less than a minute my lifelong bud Angie Mint had killed my cool image stone dead. All right, it was just her feeble idea of a joke, but boys would be talking about the day Jiggy McCue was praised for dancing the tango till they died laughing of old age. I hung about as long as possible while partners were being chosen and rejected and forced on other kids, hoping that if I held out to the very end there'd be a boy shortage and I could spend the rest of the lesson sitting cross-legged on the floor doodling in the dust. I should be so lucky. When everyone else was paired off there was just me and one boy left. A boy no girl would dance with even if he was the last one on Earth.

'Come on now, you two, don't be shy,' Mrs Porterhouse said. 'Take hold of one another and let's get started.'

I saw Pete cross his legs with delight, and sighed. 'Ah well,' I thought. I gritted Angie's teeth and grabbed Eejit Atkins by the hand. Then I slung an arm round his waist and tested the looong glide.

'Angela, you're the girl,' Porterhouse said. 'The female. Ralph is the male and the male leads. He's the one who does the long glides. What you do is drape yourself round his leg and toss your hair.'

I stared at the leg in question. 'You want me to drape myself round *that*?'

'Oh, you can do it. See how well the others are getting on. A couple of them anyway.'

I didn't care how the others were getting on. They were all trying to lead or not lead like the Argentinumians said they had to, but they didn't have Eejit Atkins's hand on their waist or have to drape themselves over his manky leg. Still, I gave it my best shot. Crash.

'Hey Wapshott, mind your stupid back! Who do you think you are – Zorro?'

As Atkins did a looong glide and twirled me

over his leg out of time to the music, he said, 'I never fort I'd be dancin' wiv you, Ange. Never in all me natural.'

It was then that I realised that Eejit had a thing for Angie. Such a thing did he have that he was grateful for whatever he could get, even a scowl or a thick ear. I noticed Trevor Fisher trying to break Mariesa Knightingale's back over his knee, and an idea came to me. A way to get back at Angie for shattering my reputation here and on the sports field.

'Eejit,' I said. 'Ralph. Will you do me a favour?'

'Sure, Ange, wot?'

'Well I really hate the name Angie, and Angela's even worse. So I was thinking, seeing as we're dancing partners now, why don't you call me something else? Something...personal.'

'Pers'nal? Like wot?'

'Special name, just between us when there's no one else about. A sort of...pet name.'

'Pet name? You mean like...Fido?'

I bit Angie's tongue to stop it exploding.

'No, Ralph, I do not mean a dog's name, I mean something soft, gentle, like, well...Sweet Lips.'

Even Atkins found this a tad hard to swallow.

'Yoo want me…t'call yoo…Sweet Lips?'

'Keep your voice down, cretin, this is between you and me.'

We did some more looong glides, abrupt halts and leg draping while he thought this over. When he'd got it all straight in his skull he said: 'Ya got yerself a deal, Ange.' He lowered his voice and winked. 'I mean…Sweet Lips.'

'But only when we're alone,' I said. 'If there's anyone else within earshot it's still Angie, right? Remember, or I'll smash your face in.'

'Cool,' he said, shooting a foot out and crippling Martin Skinner for the rest of the day.

Picturing Angie's face when she heard Eejit Atkins call her Sweet Lips for the first time, I danced the rest of the lesson away like a girl possessed. Happiest I'd been since I lost my meat and two veg.

CHAPTER EIGHTEEN

We were heading home after another hard day at school, where two of us had had to pretend to be one another while the third found it highly amusing. Turning the corner into the main square of the shopping centre we jerked to a sudden halt. In the middle of the square there's this big old tree with a railing round it, and on the lowest and biggest branch sat...Stallone. He was scoffing what looked like bird chop suey, really tucking in. Stallone's as fond of fresh bird as Pete is of chocolate.

'What do we do?' I said.

'We talk to him,' Angie said, and marched towards the tree. 'Stallone! Here, boy, here!'

Stallone looked up from his bird and snarled. Angie tried again.

'It's all right, Stal, no one's going to hurt you.'

'Meaaarrrgh,' growled Stallone.

'I don't get it,' she said as we joined her. 'He

157

usually comes to me. I wouldn't harm him, he knows that.'

'You might not,' I said, 'but he thinks you're my father's son and he isn't taking any chances in case you want to cart him back to the fruit-and-nut shop. I don't blame him. I know what it's like to suddenly be without the family jewels.'

'And I know what it's like to suddenly have them,' Angie said. 'You can take me to the vet's any time you like.'

Just then Stallone noticed me. His ears went up and the last bit of bird went down. He picked his way to the end of the branch, dropped off, and ran to me, hissing at Angie as he passed. I stooped to stroke him, but as I touched him a shiver went through him, end to end, and his back arched. He must have sensed I wasn't who I looked like. He shot out a claw and—

'Ow! You little monster!'

I whipped out a handkerchief and dabbed Angie's hand as Stallone became a blur on the far side of the square.

I thought that would be the last we'd see of him today, and I wouldn't have been sorry, but we came across him again a few minutes later as we were passing the park gates. This time he had company that wasn't in his jaws. Very unexpected company. He sat on the path some way into the park, and on a bench facing him was...

'Milo,' Angie breathed as we skidded to a halt.

We peered through the tall black railings. They hadn't seen us, just sat there looking at one another, not saying a word, even a meow, like they were in telepathic communication or something.

'First time I ever saw Stallone friendly with a non-female,' I said.

'Kindred spirits,' Angie said. 'Two unwanted waifs together.'

'Stallone's wanted. Sort of.'

'We'd better go and talk to him,' she said.

'We tried that, and look what he did to your hand.'

'I mean Milo.'

She went through the gates. Pete and I followed. We seem to spend our entire lives following Angie, whatever the body.

'Hey Milo!' she called with a cheery wave.

Milo jumped. He looked our way. So did Stallone.

We strolled towards them. For a second neither of them moved, then Stallone's tail shot up and he scooted off like he'd been fired from a catapult. Milo didn't hang about either. Instead of returning the cheery wave he jumped up and also high-tailed it.

'Ever get the feeling you're not wanted?' I said.

'All the time,' said Pete.

We continued homeward. We went to *The Dorks* first so Angie could change out of my school things. Mum and Dad weren't home yet so Pete and I dived into the biscuit tin. Should have waited until Angie had gone upstairs. She forced me to drop the handful of custard creams I'd been about to cram into her mouth.

'I don't want spots and boils all over *my* body!' she said.

I moaned of course, but said, 'OK, I'll just nibble one,' and waited till she went before stuffing even more in her gob than I'd been planning to.

I was a bit nervous. I'd been thinking about the Toilet of Doom all day, on and off. What if the sign on the toilet door said 'Engaged' again? It might be days before it would let us in for a second flush. In no time at all Angie had made me a tango king and rugby star. I dreaded to think what she might turn me into if she had my body much longer.

When she'd changed we headed across the road. The workmen had gone. So had the hole, which they'd disguised with tarmac of a different shade. In the house we found Audrey Mint looking flustered in rolled-up dungarees and a fancy headscarf. She looked like a fortune-teller who'd seen the future and didn't like it.

'Good day?' she said.

'Good day,' we said, and started upstairs.

'Keep out of Pete's room,' she called after us.

'Why?'

She pushed past us carrying a plastic basket of cleaning things.

'I'm giving it a good going over. Hoovering, dusting, polishing, removing all the sticky sweet and chocolate wrappers from under the bed. In fact generally making it habitable.'

Pete scowled. 'I like it unhabitable.'

We went to Angie's room, where we took turns facing the other way while I changed out of her school togs and Pete changed into the jeans and T-shirt Audrey threw out of his room for him. Then we went back to *The Dorks* and up to my ex-room. I wasn't going to admit it to Angie, but the six million cushions were starting to grow on me. Maybe I'd keep a few of them when I got my room back.

We sat around twiddling our toes for a while, feeling helpless. We needed to get to Pete's computer and couldn't. Frustrating. Eventually Angie told Pete to ring her mum. He refused, so she slapped him round the back of the head and did it herself.

'How's Pete's room coming?' she said into the phone. She looked at us. 'Slowly, she says.'

Slowly she said and slowly she meant. Every half-hour or so Angie phoned and the answer was always that it wasn't ready yet. Somewhere in all this my mum came home and offered to rustle up some chips, beans and sausages. We didn't refuse. The chips were great – she does really terrific chips, my mum – though the sausages could have been better. I mentioned this, forgetting that it wasn't my job to pick holes in her cooking.

'They're vegetarian,' she said.

'But we're not,' I said. 'It's like chewing grilled gerbil droppings.'

'Very nutritious.'

About half eight Angie phoned again. This time the answer was: 'Almost there. Five minutes.'

We twiddled our bits for five more mins, then recrossed the road. Twenty five minutes later we were allowed into Pete's room, which was tidier than it had been since before he moved in and smelled like the inside of a tin of polish. 'It's lost everything!' he wailed, but we didn't give him a chance to wallow in his misery. I turned the computer on and pushed him into his swivel chair.

'Toilet of Doom. Pronto.'

CHAPTER NINETEEN

The notice on the toilet door still said 'Vacant'. Good news. The door opened at a single click of the mouse. Another click activated the toilet handle and brought up the screenful of much smaller toilets with the little people walking round them. Pete flushed the people in the wink of an eye, and up it came, the thing that had brought this upon Angie and me, the Toilet of Doom itself, with its quivering seat, and:

Feel that your life has gone down the pan?
Well here's your chance to —

'All yours,' said Pete, vacating the swivel.

I glanced at Angie. She looked as edgy as I felt.

'It's got to work,' I said. 'I want my fishing tackle back.'

'It's usually called wedding tackle, Jig,' Pete said.

'Yeah, but I'm not married.'

'You don't fish either.' He smirked. He was doing an awful lot of smirking lately. 'Rugby tackle would fit, thanks to Angie.'

Angie pushed me into the chair. 'Get on with it.'

I jumped right out again. 'Oh, no, not me, not again. This time you can get all the stick if it goes wrong.'

She said something uncomplimentary, but took my place at the PC.

'Wait till I'm gone,' Pete said, sprinting to the door. 'Call me when it's over.' He closed the door firmly behind him.

'Ready?' Angie said to me.

'Not really,' I said.

She hit 'F for Flush'.

And nothing happened.

'Maybe there's a knack,' I said, 'and you don't have it.'

'I'm using your fingers.'

'Could be an attitude thing.'

'Are you criticising my *attitude* now?' she said.

'Wouldn't dare.'

She hit 'F for Flush' again. Harder.

Still nothing.

'Work, damn you, work!' she said, and hit it again. And again. And again. Nothing happened each time and she got madder and madder.

'Looks like I'm going to have to do it after all,' I said with a kindly smile.

'Over your dead body!' she said, and gave 'F for Flush' such a belt it's a wonder it didn't turn into an 'I'.

But it worked. The quivering seat flew up and the blue cloud shot out of the toilet and spread across the inside of the screen. We waited for the next bit with bated breath, whatever that is. It was still bated when the cloud started seeping into the room and, after a pause, went all sparkly.

'What's taking so long?' Pete said, lobbing his head round the door.

The cloud reached out and hauled him in. The door closed behind him like it had been kicked by an invisible foot.

'Well done, Pete,' I said, clapping softly.

Then all the little sparkly bits started going pop-pop-pop and...

'We forgot about the smell!' Angie cried. 'Why didn't you open the window?'

'Why didn't *you*?' I said.

It was hard to see through all the stinky blue sparkle but we set off towards where the door had been last time we looked – and smacked into Pete also trying to find it. There was a bit of a struggle and quite a lot of unprintable language, but we eventually made it to the landing. As we closed the door, the Toilet of Doom gave a hearty flush.

It was done. For better or worse, it was done.

Halfway downstairs we began to feel dizzy. All three of us. Pete flopped on to the sixth stair, or maybe the seventh, but Angie and I had been here before and we kept going till we reached the front door. We yanked it open and stood gratefully sucking the air out of the night.

'Feeling groggy,' she said.

'Me too. But listen, Ange, before we lose it: where do we sleep?'

'Same as last night. Case we don't switch back.'

'But if we do switch I'll wake up as me in your room and you'll wake up as you in mine. How do we explain that to—?'

'What's going on?' said Oliver Garrett, looking out of the living room where he was watching telly.

'Just going home,' Angie said, and tottered off the step.

I shut the door. 'What's up with him?' Oliver said, meaning Pete who was snoring on the stairs, face jammed between the vertical bars.

'It's been a long day,' I said. 'We had dancing.'

I crawled halfway up the stairs, grabbed Pete by the collar, and with a superhuman effort bumped him up to the top. I dropped him outside his room and opened the door – cautiously. The horrible smell was gone already and the blue cloud was shrinking back into the screen. Then, before my sleepy eyes, the last of it tumbled into the little toilet, the seat fell, and the toilet vanished.

I dragged Pete into the room. Tried to get him on the bed but my strength was going, so I left him half on, half off and staggered to Angie's room. There I reached for her stars-and-planets pyjamas, but after a bit of a fumble I gave up, crawled on to the bed as I was. Didn't even cover myself over. Then I slept. This time if I dreamt I don't remember. Maybe I was too excited to dream. Or nervous. The moment of truth was just a night away.

CHAPTER TWENTY

I woke up feeling different. More human somehow. My heart thumped. But was it my heart? I felt my hair. It was short! I jumped off the bed. I dropped Angie's jeans. I gripped the band of my fire-damaged Y-fronts. Looked inside. Tears sprang to my eyes. I was a boy again!

Creeaaak.

Someone outside the door. The sloppy grin flew off my face. Who? If it was Audrey or Oliver, what could I possibly say when they found me standing there in the wrong house, wrong bedroom, Angie's jeans round my ankles, gazing fondly into my underpants?

I tugged the jeans up and dived under the duvet. I made a little peephole so I could see out but not be seen seeing. The door opened. A face looked in. Not Audrey's though. Nor Oliver's. Not even Pete's.

No. Someone else's entirely.

Mine.

I threw back the duvet and sat on the side of the bed, staring at the me in the doorway. What was going on? I'd checked the hardware, knew I wasn't Angie any more, but how could I be in two places at once?

The other me came in, went silently to the dressing table, grabbed a little mirror, brought it to me. I looked into it. The face that stared back was not the one I expected. The one I longed to see. Far from it.

It was Pete's.

Pete's face? I had Pete Garrett's face? So did that mean...?

The phone on the landing rang. The person who looked like me – who hadn't said a word so far – went out, took the phone off the hook, brought it in, shut the door.

'Hi, Ange,' he said. 'No, it's Pete. I don't sound like Pete? Now I wonder why that is? Hey wait a minute, think I know. Must be something to do with—' he paused, then shouted '—THE COLOSSAL BOIL ON THE END OF MY STINKING ROTTEN NOSE!!!'

He clicked the phone off and drop-kicked it

across the room. It rang again almost at once. I scampered to it, picked it up.

'Angie, it's me, Jiggy.'

'Jiggy? Are you sure?'

'Not really, no.'

'Listen, if you two are pulling my whatsit...'

'Wish we were,' I said miserably.

'So what do you think happened?'

'I can tell you exactly what happened. There was an extra person in the room. A person who shouldn't have been there. A person who left his brain on the landing and came in and RUINED EVERYTHING!'

I threw the phone at Pete. I'm pleased to say he didn't duck fast enough. What had I done to deserve this? If the T of Doom could only handle one switch at a time, why couldn't it have been me who got his rightful body back? Why couldn't Pete and Angie have switched? At least they could live in their own house.

The phone was still bouncing when it rang again. I snatched it up.

'Hello!'

'Something seems to be wrong with the phone,' Angie said.

'At least it's still a phone!' I snapped.

'Look, we have to get the new show on the road. I need to be out of here before I'm seen. Bring me my school clothes. Clean ones. When you come over Pete can jump into yours and take my place here.'

This time she hung up. I didn't look at the receiver. Didn't look at Pete either. I couldn't, any more than I could speak to him. I went to his room and climbed into his school clothes (all except the underpants) while he put on jeans and a sweater. I bundled a set of clean clothes for Angie down my shirt – Pete's shirt.

'Don't get yourself seen,' I snarled. 'You don't live here today.'

'Thanks for telling me,' he snarled back.

I went down first. He crept after me. Downstairs I looked in the kitchen. Audrey and Oliver were there. She was eating Bran Flakes and banana, he was burning toast.

'Just going to see Jiggy for a minute. Back for breakfast.'

'Don't tell me,' Oliver said. 'I'm not making it.'

Pete had slipped out while this friendly chat was taking place. He crossed the road ahead of me.

I didn't bother to catch him up. I noticed that he was moving strangely, awkwardly, like a Thunderbird. It was obvious what had happened. He'd got my jigginess and couldn't handle it. He reached *The Dorks* and rang the plastic bell. I joined him on the step. I took a sneaky gander at the Boil. It was pretty nasty. No, it was *very* nasty. Huge and soft, almost transparent, sort of egg-yolky, oozing.

My father answered the door for a change. His arms were hanging more or less normally now, though I knew from his strained expression that Mum still hadn't let him off the hook about Stallone.

'Thought you were upstairs,' he said to Pete.

'New health kick,' Pete replied. 'Early morning jogs till my eighty-fifth birthday. If I don't keep it up stop my pocket money for life.'

Dad gave my bulging shirt a suspicious look, but let us in. We went up to my room. Angie was waiting for us, still in my clothes from the day before. It was strange seeing her face on her again. I'd just started to get used to wearing it myself.

She looked from one to the other of us. 'This

better not be your stupid idea of a joke...'

'Joke?' I said. 'Do you see me laughing? Angie, this is driving me insane. Right round the bend.'

'The U-bend,' said Pete sourly.

I opened his shirt and Angie's screwed-up clothes fell out.

'Well thanks a lot,' she said, picking them up and untangling them. She didn't say it through her teeth, though, like she would have done yesterday. And suddenly she was all smiles. 'You have no idea how good it is to have your own body back!'

'That's right, rub it in,' I said.

'And I feel so...*calm*. You know, all that testosterone can't be good for you. Now I know why there are so many wars. Men are basically violent. They can't help it. Have to prove they're the toughest bipeds on the block. Have to fight, or get others to do it for them. Women ought to turn on them, round them up, put them all on a great big island in the middle of nothing and burn the boats.'

'Have you finished?' I said.

'I'm just getting warmed up,' she said.

'Well later, eh? Things to do here.'

'Give me those rotten clothes,' Pete said to Angie.

'Turn the other way then.'

We looked at the wall while she got out of my clothes and put hers on.

'Where you going?' I said when Pete headed for the door with my things under his arm.

'Bathroom, d'you mind?'

'Don't give a monkey's what you do.' When we were alone I said to Angie: 'You know the worst thing about *this* switch?'

'Pete's feet?' she said.

'Pete's feet. Inside these socks are the filthiest plates in history. I could start a Great Plague by just wriggling the toes.'

'Well at least you won't have to put them in your bed.'

'No,' I wailed. 'I'll have to put them in *his*!'

When Pete returned from the bathroom there was something different about him. Something else I mean.

'Garrett,' I said. 'You evil specimen. You mutant clone of a dung-beetle. You…you…'

I ran out of insults. All I could think of was the state of my beloved face. Stare helplessly at the red and yellow lava streaming from the squashed mini-volcano on my nose.

Pete grinned. With my lips, my teeth. He said: 'I've been wanting to do that for days.'

CHAPTER TWENTY-ONE

Angie might have been glad to have her body back, but she wasn't so glad to be sitting next to Julia again. I wasn't all that happy sitting next to Pete either, specially as I had to sit in his seat and pretend to be him. When I was blamed for his useless homework I seriously thought of throttling him in public. The reason I didn't was that he was blamed for mine.

At first I kind of missed the big calm feeling that had come with Angie's carcass, but I soon got used to being without and it was kind of nice having all the right attachments back in place, even if they weren't my own. The only thing that wasn't so good was the lack of jigginess. All right, when I get agitated and start jerking around some people laugh, but that's OK. I wouldn't be me if I sat still the whole time. I mean I'm Jiggy McCue, I jig, it's what I do. I got quite envious when a couple of the teachers told Pete off for twitching while they talked. They thought he was playing up.

But we got through the morning, and by lunchtime Pete and I were just about talking again. We went with Angie to our private bench in the Concrete Garden and for once he and I ate one of the packed lunches we'd been given. Julia Frame stood behind a nearby bush waiting to be noticed and invited to join us but we ignored her, especially Angie. Over in the playground Mr Dakin was on whistle duty. He didn't whistle once, just wandered about in these sad little circles while kids beat one another up all round him.

'I feel sorry for him,' Angie said.

'Sorry for Face-Ache?' Pete said. 'Have you been at the Dr Pepper again?'

'But look at him, he's so unhappy.'

'Good.'

She wheeled on him. 'Have you no *heart*, Garrett?'

'Sure,' he said. 'Jiggy's.'

She turned to me. 'We've got to persuade Milo to go back home.'

'But we like Milo,' I reminded her.

'We still have to persuade him it's not safe

for a kid out there.'

'Have to catch him first. Don't forget, he runs from us.'

'So we run faster. He's got to go home.'

'Ah there you are, McCue, looking for you everywhere!' boomed a voice so loud and seriously macho that the Julia Frame bush squawked.

'Whatever it is I didn't do it,' I said to Mr Rice, my favourite X-Man.

'Not you, Garrett, McCue. Got some news for you!' he said to Pete.

'You're moving to another school as a dinner lady?' Pete said.

'No! You've volunteered for the school rugby team!'

'I didn't know we had a rugby team.'

'We didn't! But after Monday, when you showed what you can do, I decided to put one together!'

'When I showed what I...? Oh. Yeah.' Pete grinned at Angie and me. 'Good, wasn't I?'

'Didn't know you had it in you!' said the jolly red bozo. 'Changing room, tomorrow lunchtime, full kit!'

'Lunchtime?' Pete said. 'No, no. Lunchtime's

179

when lunch gets eaten. That's why it's called lunchtime. I know it's kind of hard to get your head round, sir, but give it a whirl, eh? Crisp?'

'Never mind *lunch*, lad! Have you no *vision*?! This could be the making of you! Do well here and you could end up representing the nation in the Baghdad Olympics! Lunchtime tomorrow, changing room, or I'll hunt you down like a mangy dog and use your bladder as a lampshade!'

The sad old headcase jogged away.

'Thanks, Ange,' I said. 'I always wanted to be Sporty Type of the Year.'

'Sorry, Jig. Got a bit carried away.'

'You should worry,' Pete said to me. 'It's not you who'll be spending tomorrow lunchtime face down in the mud.'

'Oh yes it is,' I said.

'It is?' he said hopefully.

'Yes. Because the first thing we do when we get home today is flush ourselves back in the right bodies.'

'Not if the "Engaged" sign's back we won't.'

'Think positive,' I said. 'This time tomorrow I want you sitting here happily munching and slurping while I'm out there making mud pies and a prat of myself.'

'Cool with me,' said Pete.

Suddenly Angie jumped up and yelled at the bush she'd been ignoring so well.

'Julia Frame will you leave me ALOOONE!!!'

The bush shook like it had been hit with a flame-thrower. Then there was a high-pitched sob, followed by the plicker-placker-pluck of Framish feet running into the distance. I'm glad to report I didn't feel a thing.

'Back to normal,' Angie beamed. 'Great!'

She managed to dump another admirer too before the day was done. We'd made it to last bell without any major disasters and joined the scramble for the gates. Angie was a couple of kids ahead of us when Eejit Atkins slammed his bag in the back of my legs and said 'See ya, Jig' to Pete before running on to catch Angie. He'd been sidling up to her all day, trying to get her on her own, but been frightened off by her scowl or raised hand. He obviously thought he was on a winner now school was over though because he tugged her sleeve, stood on tiptoe, and whispered something in her lug.

'Watch this,' I said to Pete.

We watched as Angie's head jerked back and she stared at Eejit in disbelief. She must have asked him to say it again because Atkins did a repeat performance. And Angie belted him.

We caught her up. 'What was that all about?' I asked innocently.

'Do you know what that little slimeball called me?' she said.

'No, what?'

It wasn't easy keeping a straight face, even Pete's, and I must have given myself away because her eyes glinted suddenly as she realised who must have put Eejit up to it.

'Hey, just a bit of fun,' I said.

'Prepare to die, McCue.'

I took a sudden right instead of left out of the gates and hoofed it.

'Another time, Sweet Lips!'

'You won't get far!' she shouted. 'Not on those legs!'

She fought her way through the gate scrum and came after me. Pete followed, shouting 'What's it all about?' He didn't get an answer.

I'd hardly gone a hundred metres before I started wheezing. Pete has about as much puff as a sixty-a-day smoker. And Angie was right about his legs. I just made it to Downmarket before they started to give way under me. I stopped, breathing hard, waiting for her to reach me and put my lights out, thanking my lucky stars that she no longer had my fists of steel. But by the time they caught up she wasn't really angry any more. I think she even saw the funny side, though she wouldn't admit it. Just gave me a little clip round the ear.

'Haven't been here for a while,' Pete said.

'Haven't missed much,' I said, gasping like a trout out of water.

Downmarket used to be the town's main street, but since the new shopping centre was built most people go there instead. Some of the Downmarket shops have gone out of business and a whole bunch of them were knocked down to make way for the block of flats for filthy-rich people. The tradesman's entrance of the flats is on the Downmarket side, but most of the windows face the other way so the filthy rich people don't have to look at the rough side of town. I peered in the laundromat, where Mum used to take me and the week's washing before she got a machine of her own. Nothing had changed. Same tatty old machines. Same old notice to the customers:

> AUTOMATIC WASHING MACHINES.
> PLEASE REMOVE ALL YOUR CLOTHES
> WHEN LIGHT GOES OUT.

We walked past the bombed-out tobacconist's, the vandalised betting shop, the little old repair shop where the lights never worked.

'*Fat Chance!* Help the homeless! Get your *Fat Chance* here!'

Angie's arm shot out and pinned Pete and me to a rubbish bin. 'Look!'

The *Fat Chance* seller stood outside the boarded-up travel agent's with a magazine bag at his feet. He wasn't like most *Fat Chance* sellers. You don't often see one in a hairy red wig and wraparound sunglasses. Most of them have a dog too. Not him. He had a cat. And the cat was...

Yep. You've got it.

We went into huddled whisper mode.

'Got to be careful how we handle this,' Angie said.

'Yeah,' we agreed.

'Delicately. With kid gloves.'

'Absolutely.'

We tiptoed from doorway to doorway till we were just one short of our quarry. Amazingly, Stallone, who has ears like a bat rather than a cat, didn't once look our way, just sat there staring at nothing like he was in Deep Thought. There was no one else about, no would-be customers, but it didn't seem to matter to the *Fat Chance* seller, who went right on yelling.

'*Fat Chance*, ladies and gentlemen! Help put a roof over someone's head! *Fat Chance! Fat Chance!*'

'Remember,' Angie whispered. 'Delicate. Kid gloves.'

We nodded.

Then we jumped him.

Dragged him into the boarded-up travel agent's doorway.

CHAPTER TWENTY-TWO

Stallone didn't hang about while we ripped his new chum's wig and glasses off. Even Angie calling his name didn't slow him down. Milo stared up at us from the ground.

'Jiggy? Pete? Angie?'

'That's us,' I said. 'Just don't ask who's who.'

'Will you get off me, please?'

We got off him but when he was on his feet Angie gripped his left wrist and I gripped his right wrist and Pete got down on one knee to grip both of his ankles.

'Why are you holding on to me?' he asked.

'Don't want you doing another runner,' Angie said.

'I can run if I want. I like running.'

'But why from us? We're your friends.'

'I have some stuff to sort out. Need to be on my own.'

'Talk to us, Milo,' I said.

'Just keep it short,' Pete said from the ground.

'I'm usually at home by now stuffing myself in front of the telly.'

'I'm not saying a word till you let go of me,' Milo said. 'Feel stupid standing here with you lot hanging on my wrists and ankles like chains.'

'We'll let go if you promise not to run again,' Angie said.

'I promise, I promise.'

We let go of him.

'What are you doing selling *Fat Chance* anyway?' I asked him.

'I have to eat. I get sixty per cent of every copy I sell.'

'Sixty per cent of nothing won't fill you out much. No one buys *Fat Chance*.'

'Well I've sold twenty-nine today.'

We all goggled in amazement. Pete got his voice back first.

'You sold twenty-nine copies of *Fat Chance*? You got sixty per cent of twenty-nine *Fat Chances*???'

'One more and I was going to knock off and go for a seafood kebab,' Milo said.

I did a quick run-through of all the things

187

regular loot like that could buy. 'Milo, how does a person become a *Fat Chance* seller?'

'Well in my case I know the bloke who publishes it.'

'The publisher of *Fat Chance* lives in our town? And you know him?'

'Yes. Yes.'

'Wow. Wow.'

'Don't you have to be sixteen or eighteen or something to sell things on the street?' Angie said.

'My friend's pretty laid back about stuff like that,' Milo said. 'I had to try and look older, though, in case the law came along.'

'The hairy red wig and wraparound sunglasses?' I said.

'Yeah. Pretty good, eh?'

'Had us fooled.'

'So what gave me away?'

'Er…'

'The cat,' Angie said. Milo looked puzzled. 'Saw him with you in the park yesterday – remember?'

'Oh yeah, right.' He smiled. 'I keep bumping into him. Some stray, I s'pose. Good cat. Very gentle, very affectionate.'

'Maybe Stallone's been Toilet of Dooming,' I said quietly to Pete. 'Swapped fur and tempers with a sweeter mog.'

'Not going by the scar on Angie's hand,' he said.

'Tell us why you ran away from home,' Angie said to Milo.

'Nothing to tell,' he replied. 'I've left, that's all.'

'You can't leave home just like that,' I said. 'I mean I think about it all the time, but I don't *do* it. Worse places than home, Milo.'

'Depends on the home.'

'Your dad's really worried,' Angie said.

He perked up a bit at this. 'He is?'

'Going spare,' said Pete happily.

'Yeah?'

'The police are combing the country for you,' I told him.

'They are?'

'Sky'll be full of helicopters any time now,' said Pete, looking up.

'Cool.'

'Where are you sleeping anyway?' Angie asked him. 'Not in one of these doorways.'

'No, not in a doorway.'

'So where?'

At this Milo came over all sly. 'Somewhere.'

'Well obviously *somewhere*,' Angie said. '*Where* is what I'm asking.'

'How do I know you won't tell anyone?'

'Milo, it's us,' I said. 'We're on your side.'

He thought for a minute. 'All right,' he said when the minute was up. 'But you have to swear you won't tell anyone. I mean *anyone*, and when I say "tell" that includes writing it down and drawing directions.'

'It's a deal.' I looked at the others. 'Right?'

'Right,' said Angie.

'Whatever,' said Pete.

Milo picked up the wig and sunglasses and stuffed them in his magazine bag. He slung the bag over his shoulder.

'It's up here.'

We parted to let him through but Angie and I crowded him all along the street so he couldn't change his mind and make a break for it.

'Here we are,' he said, stopping suddenly. We stopped too. Seemed silly not to, seeing as we were supposed to be following him.

'This is the tradesman's entrance of the luxury flats,' Angie said.

Milo smiled and fished a key-ring out of his pocket. There were two keys on it. He slotted one of them in the lock and opened the door.

'What's all this?' I asked.

He didn't answer, just pushed us inside. Then he turned a light on and shut the door.

'Where did you get those keys?' Angie demanded.

'A friend.'

'Popular all of a sudden, aren't you? Who's this one?'

'You don't need to know.'

There wasn't much to see. It was just a sort of hallway with a big plain lift. No luxuries for tradesmen.

'You sleep here?' Pete said, unimpressed.

'No, not here.'

Milo thumbed the button to call the lift. The doors sprang back.

'Get in.'

We weren't exactly delirious about this. Our friend and classmate Milo Dakin had keys to the block of flats that only filthy-rich people and tradesmen can enter, and we weren't either. But we got in the lift. Milo punched the top button on a vertical panel.

'You can't be sleeping on the roof,' I said as the doors swished shut and the lift shot up like a rocket.

'Just under it.'

The lights on the panel winked on and off like fireflies and in no time it was stopping at the top floor and the doors were swishing open. We stepped into a little hallway almost identical to the one at the bottom. It even had a door, except this one didn't open on to the street, which was probably just as well.

'Here?' Angie said.

'Almost,' said Milo.

He opened the door that didn't lead to the street. On the other side there was another little hallway, a much smarter one, with a couple of nice pictures on the wall and soft lighting, and a luxury carpet so thick it felt like quicksand. There was another lift too, but this one had doors like mirrors. And that was it, apart from one final door. The final door was made of polished wood and on it there were two words.

PENTHOUSE SUITE

In films the penthouse is always the apartment right at the top of the building, the best one, the richest one, the one with the best views and all. 'Don't tell us,' Pete said. 'You live in the penthouse.'

We had a good laugh about that. Really good laugh. We only stopped laughing when Milo stuck the second key in the door, opened it, and went in.

'What are you standing out there for?' he said.

CHAPTER TWENTY-THREE

We stepped into the penthouse like three little mice into some big old fat cat's luxury litter tray. The door closed quietly behind us. Everything about the place was quiet. In the first room, the living room, there was a luxury couch and chairs, a luxury coffee table, luxury curtains and lampshades. We wandered into the other rooms, checked out the three luxury bedrooms, the luxury bathroom, luxury kitchen, luxury fridge magnets. It was a pretty luxurious place.

I went back to the living room ahead of the others. It was hard work trudging through carpets as thick as those, but I wanted to see the view from the luxury windows which ran all along one side of the room. I've lived in this town all my life but I never had a chance to see it from so high up before. And oh boy. I had no idea we lived in such a beautiful place. Even the crummy old Old Town immediately below looked kind of nice from up there.

I heard Angie's voice, speaking in the luxury distance behind me.

'Don't you know you can be had up for breaking into rich people's gaffs, Milo?'

'I didn't break in. You saw the keys.'

'I saw them but I don't know where you got them and that's what worries me.'

'I told you, they belong to a friend of mine. He owns the place.'

'Nobody owns these flats,' I said from the window. 'They're rented out by this anonymous cove, well-known fact.'

'My friend's the anonymous cove,' Milo said.

'What?'

'He's letting me stay here because it isn't rented yet.'

'Are you trying to tell us,' Angie said slowly, 'that as well as being all buddy-bud-buds with the publisher of *Fat Chance*, you're pals with the owner of a luxury building for the super-rich?'

'Plus the evil genius who invented the Toilet of Life,' said Pete. 'Don't forget him.'

'They're all the same person,' said Milo.

'All the same...?' I said, gaping a little.

'How come you know someone who does all those things?' said Angie. She made it sound like an accusation.

'How does anyone know anyone?'

'Tell us about him.'

He shifted from one foot to the other and back again. He looked uncomfortable. Well it's not easy standing on one foot at a time.

'Better not. He likes to keep quiet about the personal stuff.'

'Milo,' Angie said. 'Anything you tell us won't leave this room – OK?'

'Unless we happen to be somewhere else when you tell it,' I said. 'Then it won't leave there instead.'

'Is there anything to eat in this dump?' Pete said. 'I'm starving.'

'All right, I'll tell you,' Milo said.

'Great,' said Pete.

But Milo didn't mean him. 'Some of it anyway. My friend started this computer games company and it made him rich. He had half a dozen cars, couple of fantastic homes, a stack of people working for him, and a wife and two kids he almost never saw.'

'Why didn't he see the wife and kids?' Angie wanted to know.

'Too busy. Not enough hours in the day.'

'Bet the wife didn't like that.'

'Not a lot. She walked out on him.'

'What about the kids?'

'Took them with her.'

'I'd have left the kids and taken the silver,' said Pete.

'It hit him hard,' Milo said. 'He sent her tickets for a no-expense-spared holiday in the Bahamas for one adult and two minors. Thought that after she'd spent some boring quality-time on a long white beach with palm trees and hammocks she'd be glad to come back and they'd live happily ever after.'

'There must be *some* grub here,' Pete said, poking about. 'Whoever heard of a luxury pad without *food*?'

'And did they come back after the holiday in the Bahamas?' Angie asked.

'No,' Milo said. 'They might have done, but...' He sighed sadly.

'But what?'

'The plane went down on the way there.'

'Went down? You mean…?'

'Everyone on board was killed.'

'Oh,' Angie said. There wasn't a lot else *to* say.

'He blamed himself,' Milo said.

'Don't see why,' said Pete, still poking. 'He only bought three of the tickets.'

'He almost went crazy. Sold the business, cars, houses, got rid of the staff. Vowed never again to care about his own comfort.'

'He owns this building,' Angie said. 'He obviously didn't give everything up if he owns all this.'

'Oh, he doesn't make anything out of this. Hands over every penny he takes in rent to good causes, helps people who need it.'

'Anonymously,' I said.

'Right,' said Milo.

'A real saint,' said Pete, wandering through to the kitchen.

'What I don't understand,' Angie said, 'is why, if your pal owns all this and lets you stay here for nothing, you have to sell *Fat Chance* to make food money.'

'He's providing a bed and shelter but I have to get my own food in,' Milo said. 'It's his only condition. He doesn't believe in free rides.'

'OK. But who is he? What's his name, where does he live?'

Milo opened his mouth, maybe to tell us, maybe not, but before he could do either Pete bounded in from the kitchen with the biggest box of chocolates you ever saw.

'Now we're *cookin'*! Can I open this, Milo?'

'Help yourself,' Milo said. 'Some woman gave them to me in the street. Very big woman. Said *Fat Chance* made her feel guilty.'

'Probably thought it was a slimming magazine,' I said.

Pete ripped the lid off and got stuck in. I groaned. My body had just lost the worst boil of its life and now all this gunge was being shovelled into it. I mean I like the odd chocolate, even a chocolate bar or three, but Pete...Pete doesn't know where to stop.

'What's up, Milo?' I heard Angie say.

Milo had slumped on to the couch. He looked pretty gloomy.

'Ah, nothing. Well yes. I sort of – stupid I know – miss home.'

'That's not stupid,' Angie said.

'Yes it is,' said Pete happily.

'I mean it's nice enough here,' Milo said, looking around. 'I can do anything I like except scribble on the walls and swing from the lights, but...you know what? This'll kill you. When I moved in the other day I threw my stuff all over the place, and then, next morning...'

Angie sat down next to him. 'You tidied up again.'

'Put it all in alphabetical order.'

'Sounds to me like you don't belong here. Be happier at home.'

'Oh, I wouldn't say *happier*.' But she'd hit the nail, you could tell.

'Your dad'll be glad to see you. He's been terrible since you left.'

'He's always terrible.'

'He's gone all quiet. Hasn't really told anyone off all week or handed out a single detention, far as I know. Walks round all by himself with his head down – like this.'

She got up and did a New Face-Ache impression around the room.

'He walks like that?' Milo said.

'Only during break,' said Pete, packing my gob.

But she'd got him. Good old Ange had twisted Milo's heart-strings, and for the next ten minutes plucked them mercilessly with tales of how sad his rotten father was, how she was sure he was a reformed character and all, till the tears were bouncing off Milo's cheeks like liquid confetti.

After that, it was just a matter of time before he was gathering up the carrier bags he'd brought from home and leading the way to the door. 'Oops, almost forgot,' he said, and went back for a thin grey case that stood against a wall. 'My friend's laptop,' he explained. 'Been looking after it for him. He asked me to take it to him tomorrow so he can shut down the toilet game.'

'He runs the Toilet of Doo – Toilet of Life from that?' I said.

'Suppose he must. He doesn't have a high-tech office or anything.'

'And he's going to…shut it down?'

'So he says. Says it's turned out to be a scientific breakthrough we're not ready for. By this time tomorrow the Toilet of Life will be no more.'

'No more...' I said faintly. Well that's it, I thought. I'm stewed. I'm going to be Pete Garrett, feet and all, till the day his heart gives out.

CHAPTER TWENTY-FOUR

Pete hadn't heard a word Milo said about the Toilet of Doom being shut down. Chocolate, that's all he was interested in. When we left the penthouse the ginormous box of chocs left with him. Halfway to Milo's he said: 'Only the orange creams left. Don't like orange creams.' He offered them round. We pulled faces. While he forced himself to scoff the orange creams I pulled Angie back a bit.

'I think we should tell him,' I whispered.

'Tell Pete he's a pig?'

'Tell Milo about the body-switch. Then he can ask his friend not to shut the T of D down till we've flushed ourselves back.'

'This isn't the time,' she said. 'Look at his little face.'

'What about his little face?'

'He's excited. He's trying not to show it, but he is. I bet he hasn't felt this keen to go home since before his mum left. This is an important moment for him. We can't throw a whole new set of spanners in his works.'

'One spanner, that's all I'm asking, just one spanner. And all he has to do is pass it on to his pal.'

'No,' she said firmly. 'We'll flush you and Pete back when we get home and that'll be an end of it.'

'The "Engaged" sign might be back by then.'

'Chance we'll have to take.'

'Funny how you're happy to take chances when it's not you that stands to lose your body for ever, isn't it?' I said.

'And you,' she retorted, 'could try thinking about someone *else* for a change.'

She rejoined Milo and jollied him along all the way home so he wouldn't get depressed again and run back to the penthouse. Pete wasn't looking too well as we approached the Dakin residence, but he valiantly polished off the last orange cream and stuffed the box in an overcrowded litter bin. It fell straight out again.

Reaching the gate we crouched behind Dakin's perfect hedge while Milo had a brief attack of nerves.

'He could lose his rag when he sees me on the step,' he said.

'He could,' Angie said. 'But you have to do this, Milo.'

'Yeah. Guess I do.'

He stood up and stuck his chest out. Lifted the catch on the gate.

'We'll stick around till you go in.'

'Thanks, Ange,' he said to her. 'Thanks, Jig,' he said to Pete. 'Thanks, Pete,' he said to me.

The gate clicked shut. He walked up the path and banged the shiny knocker. We watched through the perfect little holes in the hedge. Saw the door open, super-slow, like it was being opened by a very old lady, or a gerbil. Then there was Face-Ache on the WELCOME, WIPE YOUR FEET mat. But he was so different from the Face-Ache we knew and hated, sort of feeble and lost instead of fierce and tense. His hair was all over the place and his shoulders looked like they could use a coat hanger. The finishing touch, the cardigan and tartan slippers, made you want to call the Samaritans.

'Hello, Dad,' said Milo.

It could have gone either way. Dakin could have immediately snapped up straight and started shouting, bundled Milo inside and told him to Hoover the stairs and *do a good job*. But instead the sorrow on the old boy's phizog switched to Instant Happiness, and he grabbed Milo and...hugged him. Yes, we actually saw Face-Ache Dakin in a full-frontal man-to-boy hug. And while he was hugging he kissed the top of the poor kid's head, kissed it so many times I don't know why Milo didn't disintegrate in embarrassment.

'Touching,' Angie whispered.

'Gets you right there,' I whispered back.

'I feel sick,' whispered Pete.

Then Dakin hauled Milo inside and the door closed behind them.

'How's that for a happy ending then?' Angie said.

'Hard to beat,' I said. 'Now how about one for me? The one that has to happen tonight if I don't want to be tottering to the post office sixty years from now with a pension book marked "Pete Garrett".'

Just then there was a sound to our right. It was like someone puking. We looked towards the sound. It was Pete. Puking. Into Face-Ache Dakin's perfect hedge.

I was all for going straight up to Pete's room when we got back, but Pete was too green around the gills and slunk off to my house for a lie-down.

'Probably just as well,' Angie said. 'I mean, what's the first thing that happens after the sparkly-stinky cloud hits you?'

'You want air.'

'Yeah, but then what?'

'You get dizzy.'

'But *then* what?'

'You want to go to sleep.'

'Right. And if both of you get sleepy before tea the Golden Oldies will start asking questions. One thing we don't want is Golden Oldie questions. GOs are like dogs with bones once they get started, and before they've finished with you, you've told them every secret you ever had and most of everyone else's.'

'OK. But it has to be tonight, I don't care how sick he is.'

While waiting for Pete to get his act together

I called up the Toilet of Life. The 'Vacant' notice was still on the door. I clicked on it to stop it flipping to 'Engaged' and shutting us out. The door opened on the toilet with the graffiti and handle. I clicked the handle, the toilet flushed, and the screenful of much smaller toilets and people took its place. Of course, I needed Pete there before hitting 'F for Flush' but I wanted to be ready for when he turned up, so I started clicking around to try and flush the little people away. I clicked everywhere but couldn't find the trigger that made them yelp and dive into the toilets. It hurt to admit it but I needed Pete even for that.

We gave him an hour or two to recover, then I started ringing him. No answer for a while, but eventually the croaky voice of a very ancient person said, 'Go away, I want to die,' and he hung up. Angie snatched the phone and dialled again. This time she got in first when he picked up – with a threat to do something terrible to him if he didn't shift himself. Twenty minutes later Pete tottered over. As well as looking pretty rough he didn't look very happy. This was because he'd spent the ten minutes since he crawled downstairs being screamed at by my mother.

'Doesn't she go *on*?' he said. I asked what was up with her. 'You know your boil? You know I burst it?'

'Ye-es...?'

'Well I thought I'd never hear the last of it. Nag, nag, nag, nag. Mirror, mirror, mirror, mirror. Disgusting, disgusting, disgusting.'

I forced him into the swivel chair.

'Get clicking.'

He got clicking, but slower than usual, like every click hurt. Still, one after another the little people yelped, dived into the toilets, got flushed, and eventually the Toilet of Life came up with the banner inviting us to hit 'F for Flush'.

'Nothing must go wrong this time,' I said to Pete. 'This is our last flush. When I wake up in the morning I want to be back in my own body and no one else's.'

'You're welcome to it. Your guts are killing me.'

'Might be a good idea to open the window this time,' Angie said. She went to it, opened it. 'Neighbourhood Catwatch is off,' she said, looking out.

I joined her at the window. Across the road, my

father was leaving the house to start his nightly Stallone hunt. He was halfway along the street when a fast sleek shadow caught our eye.

'Talk of the devil,' Angie said.

'Devil cat,' I said.

Stallone, unnoticed by my dad, had jumped onto the garage roof below Pete's window and was staring up at us.

'Stallo-one,' Angie called softly. 'Stallo-one. Come to Angie. Come on, come to Angie now.'

But he didn't budge. Maybe he was thinking about it. Maybe he was trying to translate Angie's invitation into Catese. Maybe he was thick.

'Do you two animal-lovers mind if we get this over with?' Pete said. 'I need to lie down again.'

I headed for the computer. 'Yeah, let's do it. Next time I see that face I want it to be in a mirror.'

'Likewise,' he said, and hit 'F for Flush'.

'Not yet!' I said. 'Angie's still here!'

'Oh yeah, sorry.'

'He hasn't,' said Angie in disbelief from the window.

'He has,' I said, as the toilet seat flipped up.

She darted towards the door in a panic, head

down. 'You prat, Garrett. Last thing I want is to be turned into one of you losers again!'

She made it to the door as the blue cloud spread across the screen. I heard another movement behind me. Stallone had decided to accept Angie's invitation. She was just leaving as he jumped in the window and tore after her – too late. Slam. Thud. Cat skull on wood.

'That's women for you, Stal,' I said. 'Make a fuss of you when it suits them, slam the door in your face the moment the toilet seat's up.'

'Here it comes,' Pete said as the blue cloud began to seep out of the screen. He got off his chair and backed away. 'Do you think we should hold hands?'

'Not while this body has a pulse,' I said.

So we stood side by side, waiting for the cloud to cover us and do its stuff. Soon we could hardly see for blue fog, and then the sparkly bits appeared and started going pop-pop-pop, and then...the horrible smell. We palmed our noses and staggered about wondering how long we had to put up with it for it to work. I caught a glimpse of Stallone trying to climb a curtain to escape the pong, but I had enough to think about without him. When we couldn't take any more, Pete and I groped for the door. We found it, then it was behind us, closed, and we were lurching downstairs supported by the banister.

Angie was waiting for us in the hall. She opened the front door seconds before we got to it. Pete and I leaned out for a bucket or two of oxygen. Then came the need to sleep. Pete didn't hang about. He headed across the road yawning my head off. 'Perhaps I should go over there instead,' I called after him. If he heard he didn't let on, so I clawed my way back upstairs and opened his bedroom door. The cloud was already shrinking back into the computer, its work done, and you could hardly smell a thing now except furniture polish. I started groggily for the bed and tripped over something: Stallone, who'd fallen off the curtain and passed out on the floor. I dropped on to the bed so whacked that I didn't care that Pete had slept in it. Didn't care about anything actually. It was done. It was over. A few hours from now I'd be myself again.

Wouldn't I?

CHAPTER TWENTY-FIVE

Early. Very. A voice calling me. Quietly.

'Jiggy? Pete? Whichever you are, are you awake?'

A hand pinched my shoulder.

I lifted the pillow from my face and squinted up through half closed lids, hoping they were my own.

And saw Angie's face crack in two.

'It worked!'

'Really? You're not kidding me?'

But I knew she wasn't. I knew my own gorgeous voice when I heard it. She handed me a mirror. I looked into it. Kissed it. Oh, that beautiful burst boil! I was so happy I could even put up with the ache in my guts from all the chocolate Pete had shoved into them. I broke into song.

'Quiet! You're not supposed to be here.'

I was about to continue singing more quietly when I caught a movement on the far side of the bed. I peered over.

It was Pete, lying curled up on the floor. He was just waking up. And he was stark naked.

'What are you doing here?' I said. 'When did you come back, and what for? And why don't you have anything on? Don't look, Angie.'

Angie raced round and looked. Pete stared up at us from the floor. He seemed pretty puzzled himself. But then, all of a sudden, he leapt to his feet and hands, like on all fours, and jumped at Angie. Angie tumbled backwards, and before she even hit the carpet Pete was all over her – licking her face.

'Pete, you pinhead, what the hell are you...?!'

She shoved him off. Got to her feet. But he wasn't finished with her yet. He started winding himself round her legs and...purring.

'Ange,' I said. 'I don't think it's Pete.'

'Uh? Course it's Pete. Just Pete being even more of a knucklebrain than usual.'

'Look at him. Does Pete, even at his most knucklebrained, do *that*?'

He was sprawling on the floor now with his arms and legs in the air, inviting her to tickle him somewhere private. I threw the duvet over him. He seemed to like that. Started tussling with it. Attacking it.

Angie's hands slapped her cheeks. 'You mean...?'

'Yes,' I said. 'Stallone.'

'But Stallone's a *cat*.'

'Right. And he was in the room with me and Pete when we flushed the T of D last night.'

'He wasn't,' she said.

'Was. He snuck in through the window just as you left. Really put his nose out of joint that you weren't there any more. Literally.'

'But if this is Stallone in Pete's body...'

'Yes,' I said. 'Exactly. What's in my room over the road?'

I went to the window. Across the street my mother had just come out to get the milk in. A small furry creature with four paws and a tail slipped out after her. He hid behind a bush till Mum went back indoors then sauntered to the edge of the pavement, looked left and right, and, when no traffic came, stood up on his hind legs and crossed the road. With his paws over his dangly bits.

When it was time to leave for school the three of us,

in the right uniforms for a change, detoured over Milo's way hoping to bump into him and see how things were at home. I felt fantastic. Not only did I have my body back at last, but I could hardly walk in a straight line, so jiggy was I. We were almost at Milo's when we saw him and his father closing their gate and setting off for school together. Must have been the first time ever. And you should have seen them. Face-Ache's hand rested lightly on Milo's shoulder, and every now and then as they walked Milo looked up at him – and they smiled at one another.

'Never saw Face-Ache so happy,' said Angie.

'It won't do,' I said. 'You can't have someone called Face-Ache being happy.'

We followed them. At a distance. Didn't want to intrude. I noticed that as well as his school bag Milo carried a laptop-shaped carrier bag.

'Why would he be taking the anonymous friend's laptop to school?' I said.

'Maybe the anonymous friend's a teacher,' Angie said.

'A teacher? At Ranting Lane? Get real. He might not want people to know who he is, but—'

'Hey, what if it's Mr Rice?'

I laughed. The thought of the Rice Krispie being a secret Good Person who only wanted to help people...per-Rice-less!

As Milo and his old fella drew near Mr Mann's bus shelter someone shuffled past us: a downtrodden, sorrowful soul I'd never seen out of school before.

I stopped. Stared. Suddenly everything fell into place.

'What's up with you?' Angie said.

'I know who it is,' I said.

I pointed at the downtrodden, sorrowful figure trudging miserably ahead of us.

'Heathcliff? You can't be serious. I mean he's so...'

'Anonymous? Right. Mr Heathcliff is the most anonymous person in the universe. He lives in a broom cupboard without any comforts or luxuries except a little telly and three thousand dusters. What a cover! Wouldn't occur to anyone for a minute that our humble, depressed school caretaker could also be someone who builds luxury apartments, publishes a magazine for the homeless and invents dangerous interactive computer games.

It's so *obvious* once you think of it!'

'You know,' Angie said thoughtfully, 'you might just be right.'

'I *know* I am. Heathcliff's our man or my name's not Jiggy McCue.'

We started walking again so as to keep Heathcliff, Milo and Face-Ache in sight. Heathcliff surprised us a bit by suddenly shuffling into the road, but we decided he must be going to the filthy-rich apartment block.

'Wants to check everything's in good luxury running order,' I said.

He reached the opposite pavement just as Milo and Face-Ache drew level with Mr Mann's bus shelter on our side. Milo grinned at Mr Mann and gave him a thumbs-up. Mr Mann grinned back and hoicked a thumb of his own. Then, without his father seeing, Milo slipped him the laptop. I glanced across the road. Heathcliff had shuffled past the block of flats and gone into the newsagent's. You could have knocked me down with a pixel.

'What did you say your name was?' Angie said.

While I struggled to come to terms with this

unexpected twist, a man stepped out of the block of flats and crossed the road. It was the official-looking type we'd seen here before. He headed for the bus shelter and spoke to Mr Mann.

'Let's give them a listen,' Angie said.

The three of us scooted round the back of the bus shelter, where Angie and I pressed our ears to the wood and the third Musketeer rolled into a ball and licked the front of his school trousers.

'Cheque to sign,' we heard the official-looking type say. 'The donation to Kids in Need.'

'It only says fifty thousand,' Mr Mann said. 'Wallace, I told you to make it out for twice that.'

'I'm supposed to be looking after your financial affairs,' the Wallace geezer replied. 'I'm trying to stop you bankrupting yourself.'

'Let me worry about that. Tear this up and make out another – for a hundred grand.'

Wallace sighed disapprovingly. 'Well you're the boss.'

'Remember that,' said Mr Mann. 'What's the latest on the flats?'

'Just three still to be let – not counting the penthouse.'

'You can put the penthouse back on the market. My friend who was using it doesn't need it any more. Oh, and there's a *Fat Chance* vacancy. Scout around for someone who needs some money and is prepared to graft for it.'

'Yes, Mr Mann.'

Angie and I slipped out from hiding and hit the pavement on the far side of the bus shelter.

'Wait!' she said. 'We're one short!'

She dashed back for the third Musketeer, whose tongue had become quite attached to his zip.

'Morning, Jiggy McCue!' cried a hearty voice.

I turned. The man called Wallace was heading back across the road and Mr Mann was waving at me from his shelter.

'Morning, Mr Mann!'

'Thanks again for what you did the other day!'

'Any time!' I said as the other two joined me.

Angie glared at me. 'Now I ask you, is that right? Is that just? I do someone a really heroic good turn and you get the credit.'

'That's life, Ange,' I chuckled.

We turned a corner. The school was in sight. So was Jolyon Atkins and his bonehead cronies.

Spread out across the pavement waiting for us.

'Hiya, McCue,' said Jolyon.

My knees did a sudden magic trick. They turned from knees into jelly. No particular flavour.

'Care to do another heroic good turn?' I said to Angie.

'Not me,' she replied. 'I haven't got enough testosterone now to fluff up a cushion. Either grovel or take what's coming to you.'

'It should be coming to you, not me.'

'That's life, Jig,' she chuckled.

I turned. I ran. So did Angie. So did the third Musketeer, the recycled one. When at last we skidded to a heavy-breathing halt the school was once again in sight, but from a different direction and minus Atkins. The jelly between my ankles and personal places became knees again.

'So,' Angie said. 'All's well that ends well.'

'For two of us anyway,' I said, thinking of Pete, furry Pete, curled up in Stallone's basket back at *The Dorks*. My mother had been so delighted to see him (or who she thought he was) that she'd taken the day off work to wait on him hand and foot. Pete had never been treated so well. Seemed to quite like the food that went with the job too.

'Fair average, two out of three,' Angie said.

'Yeah. Could be worse.'

I threw my arm out – my very own wonderful right arm – and pointed my very own wonderful finger at the road ahead.

'Onward, Musketeers. To school!'

'One for all…' said Angie.

'And all for lunch!' said I.

'Reowl,' said the third Musketeer, and jumped up a tree after a bird.

Jiggy McCue

**Don't miss
the next exciting
JIGGY adventure...**

THE MEANEST GENIE

CHAPTER ONE

I can hardly bear to tell you this, but I have to tell someone. If I keep it to myself I'll have nightmares about it for the rest of my life, and if there's one thing I don't need in my life it's an extra portion of nightmares. It all started with the stupid genie. If the genie hadn't...

No, that's not right. It actually started with me feeling sorry for myself. Why was I feeling sorry for myself? Because I'm Jiggy McCue, the unluckiest kid in town. I'd never thought of myself as particularly lucky, but just lately luck and me had been complete strangers. I'd been held prisoner by a pair of evil underpants, and flushed down a computerised toilet. You have to admit, these aren't normal, everyday, run-of-the-mill things to happen to a person. But I had a pretty good idea why I was getting all this stuff thrown at me while it missed everyone else. It was because of what happened at the Piddle Pool the night before

I started school for the first time.

What didn't happen, I should say.

The Piddle Pool was called the Piddle Pool because it was a pool people piddled in. Boys anyway. There was this tradition in our town that if a boy weed in the Piddle Pool the night before he started in the Infants he'd have a lucky school life. I don't know what the girls did for luck, never asked, maybe they didn't need it, but boys had been widdling in the Piddle Pool for as long as anybody knew. Smelt like it too. Looked like it. There was always this dirty foamy scum on the surface, and flies all over it, licking their zzz-zzy little lips. It wasn't the sort of pool you wanted to practise the backstroke in.

Where was I? Oh, yes, the night before I started in the Infants. All the boys in my class-to-be at Ranting Lane School had gone to the Piddle Pool with their fathers or older brothers or someone. They stood in a circle round the Pool peeing long and high for luck. It was quite a moment, all those golden arcs falling into the reflected scummy moonlight while proud relatives cheered and the boys grinned happily, knowing they were going to have a really cool time at school.

Every boy except one, that is.

Me.

Because I – I alone – couldn't go.

Maybe it was nerves, having to do it in front of all those others, I don't know. I should have been able to, I'd been saving it up since way before tea. When Dad and I left the house I was cross-legged, thought I'd never make it. But what happens when it's time for the most important pee of my life? Nothing. Not so much as a trickle.

And then everyone was finished and all eyes were on me. On my useless bone dry widget. I didn't know many of the kids yet, so mostly they were strangers' eyes, which made it worse. And then...

'Whassamatter, mate, got a knot in it?'

Those words are embroidered on my heart. They came from almost-five-year-old Bryan Ryan. This was the day we met. The day Ryan became my arch-enemy. If he hadn't said those words the other kids wouldn't have picked up on them and turned them into a chant.

Whassamatter, got a knot?

Whassamatter, got a knot?

Whassamatter, got a knot?

Pee-wee-wee.

And then the water came. Not from where it should though. From a little higher up. My eyes. I turned and ran, followed by jeers and name-calling. My dad came after me, caught me up, walked me home with his hand on my shoulder. And halfway home...

I wet myself.

So that's why I was so unlucky. So I thought anyway. It was also why I'd been secretly sneaking off to the Piddle Pool every chance I got all through my schooldays, and peeing like a maniac in the hope of improving things. Hadn't worked so far, and I didn't have long to make it work. In a matter of days the Piddle Pool would become part of a car park attached to the new leisure centre being built on the site of the old brick works. I wouldn't get much luck from peeing on tarmac.

The day my latest batch of troubles started I told Mum I was going to Pete and Angie's and snuck off to the Piddle Pool instead. Nice day. Big fat sun, brilliant blue sky, fluffy-wuffy little clouds. I took up my usual position beside the Piddle Pool. Just across the scummy water was the almost-finished leisure centre. Over to one side was all that was left of the brickworks – three tall thin chimneys that no longer smoked. No one about. I unzipped, flipped out, shut my eyes, got down to business. I'd hardly started when a chilly wind ruffled my hair and pumped my shirt. I opened my eyes. And gasped. Six seconds earlier the world had been all bright and warm. Now it was all gloomy and chilly, and there was a little black cloud parked directly over my head. Then two terrifying things happened, one after the other. First a great puff of purple smoke shot out of one of the dead brickworks chimneys, then lightning sprang from the little black cloud above my head. The lightning struck the Pool right in front of me – kerzoom! kerpow! kerpat! – and the scummy water started churning and bubbling like there was something huge down there that was seriously thinking of leaping out and turning my throat to marmalade. My hair stood on tiptoe, my spine became a jigsaw with a piece missing, and I suddenly thought of several other places I'd rather be. Like my bedroom, with a chair against the door.

I spun round. I picked up my feet. I skedaddled.

To get home from the Piddle Pool I had to pass the library, my school, and Butch & Betty's Unisex Hair Salon. I don't do a lot of running, think it's bad for your health, and I reckoned it must have showed because people kept pointing at me, girls giggled, and a couple of nuns covered their eyes, as if running without practice was a mortal sin or something.

When I shot through the front door of *The Dorks* (our house) the first person I met was Dad, on his way in from the garden for a beer.

'If that was mine I'd put it away, Jig,' he said. 'If your ma sees it she'll probably have you arrested.'

'What are you on about?' I said.

He looked at the front of my jeans. So did I.

And groaned.

No wonder people had pointed. No wonder they'd giggled and covered their eyes. I'd run all the way home from the Piddle Pool with my flies open, and everything – the whole kit and caboodle – had been…

No. I can't say it. Just thinking about it makes me sob into my fist.

CHAPTER TWO

Three weeks earlier, Mr Dent our Woodwork teacher had given us a project. 'Construct something,' he said. 'Anything you like, use your imagination.'

'Imagination, sir?' This was me. 'You mean instead of wood?'

'If I had enough wood, Mr McCue,' he replied with a wooden smile, 'I'd use *my* imagination to build an escape-proof cell for you lot.'

'Ah, but then I'd use *my* imagination to escape, wouldn't I?'

'And how would you do that, seeing as I wouldn't have equipped the cell with tools for you to escape *with*?'

'Simple. I'd use Ryan's head as a battering ram. Nothing more wooden than that.'

Ryan snarled at me. I waved some spare fingers at him across the class.

By the end of Week Three most of our projects

were finished. I was quite pleased with mine. Very pleased actually. Mr Dent patted me on the shoulder, and some of the others said nice things. Not Pete though. It would kill Pete to be impressed by anything I do.

'A kennel,' he said. 'Brilliant, seeing as you haven't got a dog.'

'We were told to make something out of wood, not something a dog would live in.'

He held his effort up proudly. 'At least mine's useful.'

'Useful? Pete, it's an ashtray.'

'So?'

'Well for one thing no one in your house smokes. For another it's made of wood. Leave a ciggy smouldering in that and you'll be over a fireman's shoulder before you can burp twice.'

Suddenly there was this great whooping, laughing, cheering sound. A crowd had formed around the benches on the other side of the room. Pete and I went to check it out. Couldn't see a thing till we'd torn some shoulders apart and forced our way through. When we got to the front I immediately wished we'd stayed at the back, because the thing that was getting everyone so worked up was Neil Downey showing off his woodwork project – a little guillotine. The guillotine on its own would have been OK, but Downey was putting it to work, which wasn't so OK. He was executing maggots. He'd brought in a tin of the things, thousands of them, all white and wiggly. No one wanted to touch them, and no one did except Downey, who just dipped in, no gloves, no tweezers, picked one up, dropped it in place. His guillotine had a razor blade on this pulley sort of thing that came down at the flick of a switch. Splat! Maggot in two halves, still wriggling. It was horrible. Disgusting. Downey had never been so popular.

Not with me, though. I have this thing about squiggly-wiggly things. When we were little, Pete would spend hours pulling worms out of the ground to see how far they'd stretch before they snapped. I used to get physically sick just watching. I mean literally throw up. And that was just garden worms. I'd probably turn to a quivering heap of jelly if I ever met a snake on a dark night. Spiders, fine. Rats, no big deal. But put me next to a squirmy creature like a snake or a worm – or a maggot – and I almost pass out. I didn't pass out the day Downey brought his tin of maggots in and turned them into small twins, but it was a near thing. I certainly gulped a bit. I grabbed hold of Pete to keep from falling to my knees, but he shook me off. So I dropped to my knees anyway, backed out through all the cheering legs, and staggered over to the window for some lungfuls of pure clean maggotless air.

After school we had to take our woody masterpieces home. No problem for someone with an ashtray or a baby guillotine, less of a breeze for a kennel king. Normally I'd have asked Pete and Angie to help, but Pete had detention for copying my Maths homework error for error, and Angie was at Miss Weeks' Kick-Boxing For Girls Workshop. So I set off alone, kennel on shoulder. I didn't fancy carrying it through the crowded shopping centre, so I did a detour down Effluent Lane. This wasn't a short cut, but there are no shops in Effluent Lane, so you don't see too many people looking for stuff to buy. The kennel was quite heavy and I kept having to stop and put it down, or change shoulders, but in the end I found the best way to carry it was on my back, like a big wooden hump.

I came to the bit of land where the brickworks used to be and the new leisure centre almost was. Passing the Piddle Pool I remembered what happened yesterday. It didn't seem so scary, looking back. Sort of a freak weather thing. Well, the cloud and lightning part. I didn't want to think about the suddenly puffing dead chimney. I decided to take a good-luck leak as I was there. I set the kennel down beside the Piddle Pool, unzipped and took aim. I kept my eyes open this time.

Tinkle, tinkle, tinkle. (That was me.)

'Right. A thousand and one. Here we go.' (That wasn't me.)

You have to picture this. There I am standing on the bank of this stinking old pool, dogless kennel at my side, one hand on hip, the other not, when the stuff I'm peeing into leaps up like a great wave, then comes back down and drenches me all over. I didn't need reminding to zip up this time. Zipped so hard I almost broke my jaw. Then I stood gasping and dripping, wet clothes clinging, yellow piddle scum on the end of my nose. My eyes were waterlogged, so I had to blink hard to see, and what I saw sent me into an immediate jig.* I was no longer alone. A teenager with dreadlocks and no shirt stood waist-deep in the Piddle Pool. And he was speaking.

'Your wish is my command, O...'

He paused after 'O', and his mouth twisted, like his lips were wrestling with one another, but finally said, through his teeth:

'*Master.*'

'What?' I spluttered, jigging around and spitting ancient pee.

'That's you,' he said.

'What's me?'

'You summoned me, which makes me your Humble Servant. Don't let it go to your head, it's just one of those dumb things we have to say. I don't do humble.'

'My servant?' I said, wiping my face on my sleeve.

'I'm a genie,' he said, swiping at some flies. '*Your* genie. That means I have to obey you, like it or not. If I refuse, I go straight back where I came from, and let me tell you I could do with a break from here.'

'Whoa,' I said. 'Back up. Genie? You're a genie? *My* genie? You have to obey me? *Me*? Jiggy McCue, unluckiest person on the planet?'

He took a step towards me in the scummy water. I took a step back. Someone who snorkels in urine is more likely to be a dangerous psychopath than a genie.

'Relax,' he said. 'I won't hurt you. I'm here to make your dreams come true. With wishes.'

'W-wishes?' I said, twitching wildly. This was getting serious.

'Wishes. Three. You just won the Piddle Pool lottery, kid.'

Read the rest of
The Meanest Genie
to find out what happens next!

MICHAEL LAWRENCE

JIGGY'S MAGIC BALLS

A MEDIEVAL MESS!

Jiggy's medieval life is one dirty dung heap of trouble after another. Worse, he has to work for the dumbest Knight in the land, Sir Bozo de Beurk. But when Jiggy discovers a pair of magic balls, his fortunes might be about to change...

In stores and online NOW!

'Joust Hilarious!'
The Daily Chain Mail

978 1 40830 803 5 £5.99 PB
OUT NOW!

www.jiggymccue.com

Do you think you're funny?

Fancy yourself as a published author?

Send us a joke that would make Jiggy McCue laugh and it could feature in a Jiggy McCue book!

Email your joke to jiggy.jokes@jiggymccue.com or send it to us at Jiggy Jokes, Hachette Children's Books, 338 Euston Road, London NW1 3BH

Don't forget to include your name and age!

Here are some of our favourite jokes so far...

I've always had an overactive imagination. Like the time I found myself drowning in an ocean made out of Tango. It took me a while to work out it was just a Fanta-sea!
Chelsie Coghlan, 10, East Sussex

What is smelly and sounds like a bell?
DUUUUUUUUUUUUNNNNNNNNNGGGGGGGGGGGGG!!!!!!!
Hollie Robinson, 10, Hertfordshire

How do you get Pikachu on a bus?
Poke-m-on!
Caleb Andrews, 6, Bucks

What did the inflatable Headmaster say to the inflatable boy who brought a pin into the inflatable school?
'You've let the school down, you've let me down and most importantly — you've let yourself down!'
Ella Davis, 12, Surrey